TAKING ON A GIANT

Newlands saw that his game was not yet quite won, nor Beatrice, perhaps, wholly lost to him, and even amidst the cheering the crisis came.

Big Georgeson rose and stalked forward. "Wait a minute, boys," he called. "What has he given us now but a lot of hot air? That's what I'm asking you."

The crowd turned to the new speaker with almost as much interest as they had paid Newlands. The latter saw that he must shut up this speaker at once. If he failed, he was lost and could never get the power back.

Newlands strode to the orator and smote him heavily upon the shoulder. "Georgeson," he roared, so that every man in the room could hear him, "you're a quitter and a yellow dog!"

Georgeson turned and glowered at Newlands. Tall as the latter was, he was overshadowed by this giant.

"You're a quitter," repeated Newlands steadily, "and a yellow dog!" He pointed his words by striking Georgeson with his open hand across the cheek. The blow sounded through the room like the crack of a whip.

MAX BRAND®

THE LONE RIDER

LEISURE BOOKS NEW YORK CITY

A LEISURE BOOK ®

January 2005

Published by special arrangement with Golden West Literary Agency.

Dorchester Publishing Co., Inc.
200 Madison Avenue
New York, NY 10016

ISBN 0-8439-5439-6

The name "Leisure Books" and the stylized "L" with design are
trademarks of Dorchester Publishing Co., Inc.

Printed in the United States of America.

Visit us on the web at www.dorchesterpub.com.

THE LONE RIDER

Chapter One

ONE HUNDRED THOUSAND DOLLARS

If Newlands was frequently in the public eye, it was equally true that he was quite as often out of the public eye. He attracted notoriety without effort, but he baffled too inquisitive reporters with equal ease. Consequently, although every city editor in San Francisco was continually taking Newlands's stories across his desk, he was never entirely satisfied, but kept watching and waiting for the Newlands story that should furnish the key to the mystery.

Society knew him as a clever host, an original entertainer, a brilliant guest, and a dilettante in music. The result was that he was much sought after, and, if he was rather seldom found, it made his appearances more attractive. His frequent disappearances lent him the needed touch of mystery and made him a celebrity. After one of these disappearances he had turned up at the Olympic Club and won the heavyweight amateur championship of the West Coast with a well-timed right cross that put Kid Farwell to sleep in the last of the fifth. On another occasion, after a two weeks' absence, he was identified as a labor agitator, and to his speeches was attributed a teamsters' strike which tied up the heavy traffic for nearly a month. But it was thoroughly believed that he took part in diversions of a more disreputable character than these, and what feminine society did not know, it exaggerated with dark hints.

It would seem that so varied and unusual a reputation would have brought content and the lasting response of good humor, but as Newlands sat in his library, he was far from content. In the dusk of the late afternoon the street lamps twinkled. Over the Bay the light on Alcatraz Island began to wink, the ferry boats moved with the reflection of their own illumination by their sides, and now the last flash of the sun ran in a wave of twinkling golden fire on the far-away windows of the Berkeley hills—the last stir of life before the long hush of the night.

But William Newlands was ill at ease. He studied this new old change with a frown, and then turned with his fingers drumming on the arm of his chair. As he turned, the faint light from the windows blocked out the lines of his face in shadow, a striking face with its thick, handsome lips, square chin, and the short-cropped black mustache, and above all the peculiarly animated light of his eyes, forever shifting and changing. Five years before every feature had been clearly cut, but now the dense hair coming somewhat too low upon the forehead, and the over-fullness of the flesh about the lower part of the face suggested the matinee idol that had gone into moving pictures with a press agent.

A light tapping came at the door.

"Yes?" said Newlands.

The door opened on a sallow-faced, slender man.

"Mister Munroe, sir, and your mail."

He advanced slowly and laid a handful of letters on the edge of the desk.

"Show him in, Benedict," Newlands said without looking up.

Benedict hesitated for a moment, as if he were about to speak, and kept his eyes somewhat backward, toward the door. Then, as if he had changed his mind or was dropping some trouble or doubt about it, he shrugged his shoulders slightly and turned away.

As the servant withdrew, Newlands rose and started to pace the room. He stopped by the desk and commenced to shuffle the letters one by one. He continued this even after Munroe stepped into the room, but the latter seemed oblivious to the lack of a greeting. He busied himself with his gloves, and finally tossed hat, coat, and cane upon a chair, and seated himself within the light of the lamp. He was tilted back somewhat in his chair with the tips of his fingers brought together under his chin.

In every respect except one he was the exact physical opposite of Newlands. He was framed for elegance rather than strength, a long, narrow face, and tapering fingers suggestive of extreme agility. The one similarity between the two lay in the fact that their eyes were lighted with the same peculiar animation forever shifting and changing, even when the face was exposed.

"I got your message while I was in Stockton," began Munroe, after he had studied the expression of his host for a few moments, "but I had to go on to Fresno on a hurry call from your Edgerley Packing Company people."

He lowered his head to watch Newlands more closely as he said this, but the larger man shrugged his shoulders and made no other sign.

"Getting restless again, chief?"

Newlands threw the letters away from him with a sudden movement of disgust, and started to pace up and down the room with long, irregular strides. A shadow of a smile crossed Munroe's face and was gone again as fleetly as it came.

"Everything is dead!" burst out Newlands at last. "Nothing happens, nothing. Good God, man, I'm getting to be as dead as the rest of the world I see. And what do I see? The same faces! The same town! The same . . . oh, the devil take it all!"

"Sort of out of tune with things?" said Munroe.

Newlands faced him with a frown. "Yes," he said slowly, "I've always been out of tune. There's no reason for it. I have enough ability. And yet I lean on you. I have more than the usual ability, I know."

"Yes," agreed Munroe, "God gave you enough of everything except a conscience. Go on."

Newlands threw back his head and laughed pleasantly. "Conscience? Bah!" He sobered and stared down at the floor. "Somehow I can't get along without you, Munroe. You're like dope, like morphia. You've gotten into my blood, and I need you. Otherwise, I lose my appetite for life."

"Don't exaggerate," Munroe chastised, waving a graceful hand in the air as if he pushed aside an unpleasant thought. "I never lead. I merely suggest. I give the start. After that, there's nothing in heaven or hell, my dear fellow, that could lead you."

Newlands turned and squared his shoulders at him. "Out with it," he said. "What's on your mind, Jimmy? Whenever you come here with a manner smoother than oil, I know there's some hell up. What is it? Can I get in?"

"You're already in," grinned Munroe.

"Well?"

"The Edgerley people are about to investigate their books."

"They are about to what?"

"Add up a few totals," Munroe said placidly, "and then they'll find they're just about forty thousand short. Got that much in the bank, dear boy?"

"Not half of it," growled Newlands, and then somewhat dazedly: "President Kerr said he'd turn everything over to me without question as his broker and not ask for an accounting for six months."

"Kerr was overruled by the executive board."

"Why didn't you tell me before?"

"He is sending word by me."

"Bah!" snapped Newlands. "I'll make a trip down to Fresno tomorrow and talk with those directors. I'll bring 'em to time. Some fool has been talking."

"No good," answered Munroe, "they mean business. It'll be a month before they find out the exact state of the firm's affairs. It's a long time."

"If they make it two months, I could realize on the G and W stock," said Newlands.

"If." Munroe smiled.

Newlands glanced quickly at him and scowled. "Well?" he asked.

"I suggest travel," said Munroe.

"You're a quitter, Jimmy," sneered Newlands. "Sit down and let your wits travel for you. I tell you this doesn't bother me. It merely warms my heart to have a problem that's worthwhile."

"Worth about ten years," agreed Munroe.

"Rot!" said Newlands. "Sit down there and do a little thinking while I finish this mail, then I'll join you and we'll fix this thing up in ten minutes."

Munroe sat perfectly still with one pale hand laid across his eyes, but Newlands was humming as he ripped open letter after letter. Some he tossed back upon his desk, but the majority he crumpled and dropped into the wastepaper basket at his side. At last he apparently came to one of an unusual character. The humming stopped, and a frown gathered as he

11

read. He fell back in his chair wearily, and the hand holding the letter dropped at his side.

"What's the matter," asked Munroe, who seemed to be almost hypnotically aware of the movements of his companion, "some relative died?"

"The game's up," sighed Newlands, "indefinitely postponed. Close up shop and pack your grip. There's nothing doing now. I guess my prayer is answered, all right. I've got my hands full." He groaned and closed his eyes.

"Heads up!" snapped Munroe. "It can't be as bad as that."

"Bad?" Newlands cried, sitting up suddenly in his chair. "It's worse! It's hell itself! Do you know what I'm going to be? You don't. It can't be guessed. I'm to become a girl's chaperon, a sort of semi-female companion, a guiding light of the afflicted . . . me!"

"You're delirious," said Munroe with concern. "This is a holdover! Let's hear the news."

"Listen," Newlands said, and he commenced to read from the letter.

Dear Mr. Newlands,

Before my father died, he left me this letter, sealed and addressed to you, and told me to mail it to you at once. So I am sending it on to you.

What may be in the letter I can only guess, but I know that he wanted me to go to San Francisco as soon as I had seen to his burial in Honolulu, and he wished me to look you up when I reached that city.

I am glad to leave Honolulu. The house where Dad and I have lived together all these years is too full of painful memories to me now, and, since he wished me to go to the mainland, I intend to sail on the *Sonoma* on the third, and will land in San Francisco on the 9th of June.

As soon as I land, I shall communicate with you.

Yours,
Beatrice Crittenden

"Nice, isn't it?" went on Newlands. "But that's just the beginning. That's the matter of the approaching storm, Jimmy, dear. Here's the real thunder and lightning, and every stroke falling on my poor defenseless head."

He raised the letter and commenced to read again.

Dear Billy Newlands,

I reckon you won't remember me, but I recollect when you were a tolerable little shaver. I used to be a pal of your dad's. I suppose you've heard him speak of me.

Well, it happened that once, when your dad and I was running a trader down in Samoa in the early days, that I done him a favor which he didn't never forget. I'm reminding you of that favor now, not because you inherited your father's obligations, but because I'm hard put to it to find the right sort of a friend just now.

I don't need help for myself, but for my girl, Beatrice. The doctor tells me that I'm due to die any day, and I'm writing this letter to you, which Beatrice will mail after my death. I want to get it off my mind, because a frisky heart don't stop by the clock.

I don't need any help for Beatrice. She'll have close to a hundred thousand in the bank. But I want to send her away from these islands. I want her to go to the States. I want her to know the best sort of folks over there. And I know you'll take care of her for me. You won't mind when you see Beatrice, because she's so human, more human than any other woman I've ever known, saving her mother before her. Everybody loves Beatrice, because she's as square as a man and as simple as a boy. Most of all, simply because she's Beatrice.

So I'm sending her to you, my boy, because I knew your dad so well, and because I must have her with someone I can trust. I haven't heard of you for a long time, but I know the son of old Fighting Joe Newlands must have the right stuff in him. Treat her like a sister, boy, and you'll know that an old man is asking God to bless you for it.

Yours truly,
Daniel Crittenden

Newlands dropped the letter and groaned again.

"It's hard, all right," sighed Munroe.

"Hard?" Newlands said. "That isn't the right word. You've got to go into the Indian dialects to find the right word for this."

"How old is she?" asked Munroe.

"I don't know," he replied wearily. "I think I heard my father speak of her years ago. She must be eighteen or nineteen or twenty now. It's all one."

"One hundred thousand dollars," Munroe said dreamily.

"And I'm elected to run a perambulator and be a combination trained nurse and fireless cooker!"

"One hundred thousand dollars!" repeated Munroe.

"Munroe . . ."—Newlands frowned—"hands off here! You may be a yellow dog, but I still have a few of a man's instincts left to me."

"One hundred thousand dollars," Munroe said again.

"You're hypnotizing yourself," said Newlands. "I tell you there's nothing doing here. Get out. You make me sick all the way through. Do you think I'm a cradle robber?"

"Newlands," Munroe suggested, "let me take this burden off your hands. Let me run the perambulator. You've no idea how gentle my touch is. I love children."

Newlands grinned broadly at him. "Yes, Jimmy," he said, "your touch is so soft that she wouldn't feel her purse slide away. Not a word. 'More human than any woman I've ever known, saving her mother!' Don't you see what that means? One of those Janes with a disappearing chin and a quivering smile. Drinks Postum and sleeps with a hot water bag. Has pale eyes and. . . ."

"One hundred thousand dollars," murmured Munroe. "Hmm." He rose slowly and passed a careful hand across his hair. "Newlands," he went on, "I have a hunch that you'll follow this further than you say. Remember that I'm an old pal. Let me in on it."

"Run along." Newlands laughed. "I don't like soft meat even when I'm tigerish. The girl's safe with me, all right. Don't leave town, Jimmy. I'll need you yet on this Edgerley deal. I'll take her to an orphan asylum or an old ladies' home and then meet you again. Stay where I can get you by phone tomorrow."

"It's all like a fairy story," murmured Munroe dreamily. "I can't believe it. Just when you face a ten-year vacation."

"Nonsense," said Newlands. "I can get by that game."

"The city editors like you so well," went on Munroe. "Think of the scare-head on the *Examiner* . . . 'Society man embezzles funds of widows and children!' Lots of small investors in the Edgerley, Newlands."

"Damn you, Munroe," Newlands said softly.

"And here comes this gift from the gods," pursued his

15

companion gently, as if he had not heard the comment. "Here comes one hundred thousand beans sewed up in a little sack with gilt ribbon. Too bad it isn't Christmas time. I suppose you'll get her a room at your old friend *Madame Fenwick's*?"

"What a hound you are," muttered Newlands. "No. Go to Avery's tomorrow morning and reserve a suite for Miss Crittenden, one of the best."

"Avery's?"

"Yes."

"That's perfectly respectable, man. You could never pull a little game there."

"Exactly. Do as I say. I've made up my mind, Jimmy. Not if I have to spend twenty years in jail."

"One hundred thousand dollars." Munroe sighed. He gathered up his hat and coat, and, as he reached the door, he turned and raised one hand. "William Newlands," he said with ministerial solemnity, "the good Lord keep you out of temptation."

Chapter Two

FIGHTING JOE NEWLANDS'S SON

It was, in fact, a case that needed divine intercession. In the face of an auditor, Newlands could pretend indifference to a certain extent, but in the loneliness of human calculation he knew that Munroe was right, and that he stood face to face with a crisis that promised ruin both to his social position and to his financial prospects unless he saw a sudden way to the light. The appeal of old Daniel Crittenden rang in his ears, but it did not ring more loudly than Munroe's reiterated "one hundred thousand dollars." The girl was an abstraction. The relief that her money suggested was a very vital reality.

But on the 9th of June a chill fog muffled everything except the clanging noises of the waterfront, the rattle of drays, and the shouting of express men and hotel bus drivers, as he stood on the pier waiting for the *Sonoma* to swing into her pier.

He had tipped a longshoreman a dollar to run up the plank as soon as the boat made dock, and given him another dollar to tip the steward to locate Beatrice Crittenden and bring her to him. He watched the boat draw near into her pier an hour late and snuggled vainly into his coat collar to find warmth, dreaming the while of the comfortable bed where he might have pursued his usual slumbers at that hour of the morning if it had not been for a woman.

He shrugged his shoulders and watched his longshoreman

run blithely up the gangplank. In time he saw the long-shoreman walking down the gangplank, carrying two suit-cases, and before him walked a girl. Newlands forgot his coldness and sleepiness. If it had been anyone save him, one would have said he had begun to stare. He shouldered his way into the crowd.

"This is the guy," boomed the longshoreman's bass. "This fellow here."

"You are Mister Newlands?" said a voice. "I am so happy to find you!"

Newlands palmed the longshoreman a five-dollar gold piece. There are voices and voices in this world, but there is no sound to touch the strings of a man's heart like the con-tralto voice of a woman, throatily vibrant, the controlled, low voice of a woman of culture.

"I am William Newlands," he was saying, as he took the firm hand of this level-eyed vision into his own. "I'm glad to take up a friendship where my father left off."

He picked up the suitcases and followed her through the crowded pier. Now and then she smiled back to him with some remark, but on the whole he was grimly studying the poise and alertness of her step, and the little transparent fluff of hair at the base of her neck.

He directed the chauffeur to go to Avery's.

Jimmy had, as usual, done his artistic best in the selection and appointment of the apartment. In the brief time allotted to him, he had secured a Negress, who now bustled about the place preparing chocolate in a beautiful china service. In a vase of faintly tinted crown glass in one corner of the room a spray of long carnations already lent a touch of fragrance.

She thanked him, her eyes brimming with sudden excite-ment like a boy's, and Newlands choked and growled and grew crimson as he thought of Munroe's purpose in this elaborately arranged greeting.

It was partly to cover his embarrassment that he fled from the apartment house. He told her that he would leave her to rest that day, and in the evening he would call to take her to supper. He gave her his telephone number on his card and asked her to call for him in case she wanted to know anything that he might tell her.

He knew instinctively that the artful Munroe would be waiting for him when he reached his house, and he both dreaded and wished to see him, but when he found him comfortably ensconced behind a magazine and puffing slowly on a long cigar, he felt an unreasoning anger come over him. He walked to him, leaned over, laid a large hand on the pale forehead, and pressed back his head.

"It wouldn't strain me much to press that head a little farther back, Jimmy," he said at last, after he had studied those uncertainly lighted eyes for a time. "A little farther back and the bone would break, eh, Jimmy boy?"

Munroe regarded him without emotion until the hand was removed, and then he shook his head in mock wonder. "What a poet you are, Newlands," he breathed. "Something terse and . . . er . . . Browningesque about you."

With a strange mixture of delight and fascinated fear he watched the muscles gather to a little ridge along Newlands's jaw. Ever since he had known Newlands, it had given Munroe endless pleasure to torment his companion. When he was far away from the man, he often was afraid that he might one day go too far, but when he was with him, he was continually irritating him in a thousand ways to which he had discovered the large man was susceptible. It was like an active panther playing with a tiger, and never knowing when his more sluggish but far more dangerous companion would unsheathe his claws and cuff him into oblivion, yet he continued the difficult game, always hoping that he could trust to his brains and his agility to escape from the ultimate conflict.

In fact, all of his relations with Newlands were colored by strange admixtures of conflicting sentiments. He respected his friend's mind and his ability to execute dangerous affairs coolly and efficiently. He admired his power, but he was inclined always to despise a certain headlong rashness with which Newlands plunged into events. He disliked and condemned his friend's gambling spirit. He himself had long been a professional gambler, and merely because he had long ago discovered that he could trust his brains and discretion further than most other men could trust theirs. But Newlands was possessed of the true love of chance, which gives an added zest for life to so many strong men. Feeling that he knew the strength and the weakness of Newlands, Munroe knew that by diplomacy he could always exercise a controlling force over him, and yet the game was dangerous.

Newlands had turned and walked to the far end of the room. He stood with his back to Munroe, in a characteristic attitude when he was thinking deeply. His head was bowed somewhat, and the bulging shoulders forced back almost painfully, while his hands were clutched hard behind him. It thrilled Munroe to the heart to think that it lay in his power to start this great force in one direction or another.

"And the girl, who is more human than anyone except her mother before her?" he queried lightly.

He could see the hands tighten their grip upon each other. For a moment he feared to pursue the subject further, but he had made up his mind hours ago that he would put this thing through, and now he was merely fencing to discover the right course to tempt Newlands. He waited till the hands relaxed, studying his man the while with a somewhat sinister smile under the light drumming of his fingertips.

"It was a pretty hard job to get that apartment ready," he went on in a more friendly voice. "I didn't even know her complexion. From the letter, I thought she might want a Mother Hubbard and a box of daisies to make her feel at home. Tell me about her, Billy . . . when she got in the rooms, did she gurgle and say . . . 'How perfectly delicious!' . . . or did she act reasonable? Tell me about her, man."

Newlands turned and commenced pacing the room. "Tell you about her?" he questioned, but he spoke not so much to Munroe as to himself. He stopped and threw his head back, frowning contemplatively. "Why, Munroe, she's real . . . she's what her father called her . . . human. I don't know whether she's beautiful or not . . . singular voice."

He sat down as if to order his thoughts more clearly. "Strange voice!" he broke out again. "Has a sort of purr to it, a dim, childish, velvet touch that goes right inside you. Perfectly frank eyes. Hmm. Shakes hand like a man, and yet not effusively."

"You're a poet, all right," said Munroe. "Go on, my boy . . . you'll marry her at this rate. By the way," he went on in a casual voice, "I got a telegram this morning, in code."

He passed the telegram to Newlands and sat back to wait.

Directors suspicious; insist books be examined immediately; warn Newlands. Kerr, read Newlands.

He crumpled the slip of paper and stared a moment straight ahead of him before he raised his eyes to Munroe. The glint in them made the latter stir in his chair.

"Why didn't you show this to me before?" asked Newlands.

"Didn't want to spoil your little party today," Munroe replied glibly. "Besides, you have a month before they can get any real information as to conditions that involve you."

A little silence came on them.

21

"And it's only forty thousand dollars," Munroe added.

"It might as well be a million, the way I'm fixed now," said Newlands.

"One hundred thousand dollars." Munroe sighed.

He knew this was the crucial moment. If he had made the move too soon, he knew that Newlands would be through with him forever, and he watched with an ill-concealed concern as the big man half turned, in his chair, with one large shoulder jutting forward. But he had judged rightly. Newlands sank back in his chair and covered his eyes with one hand.

"Just for the sake of supposing, Jimmy," he said gruffly, "tell me what your idea of the game may be."

"Well," murmured Munroe, "I'm perfectly content with twenty-five thousand, and that leaves you seventy-five to meet the Edgerley people and . . . and go on the honeymoon."

"My God, Jimmy," said Newlands, "do you think I'm going the limit in this thing? Do you think I'm going to marry the girl, even if she'd have me?"

"Marry?" queried Munroe with a sardonic smile. "Tut tut! I'm not talking in my sleep, Billy, my boy. Newlands . . . bachelor Billy Newlands . . . married? Rot! Of course, I don't mean a real marriage."

"Well?" said Newlands with a slight shudder, as if he refused to let his mind go to the conclusion to which Munroe pointed.

"In the first place," went on Munroe, warming to his plan as he spoke, "you take her to *Madame* Fenwick's and get her a fine little suite of rooms. In the second place, you commence a little campaign such as only you can carry out to perfection, Newlands. She'll see nothing but you, talk to no one but you, and dream of nothing but you, and then one fine day you have a little heart-to-heart talk with her and tell her that you have all your life dreamed of some girl, and that, when you saw her, you knew the dream had at last come true. She'll fall for it. They all do, my son. Then. . . ."

"Yes?" Newlands urged softly.

Munroe rose and swiftly passed a black scarf around his throat, buttoned his coat higher, and drew his hat down over his eyes, at the same time pulling out the lines of his face to an unworldly solemnity. He raised a hand and turned his eyes upward.

" 'Whom God hath joined . . . ,' " he began in rolling tones.

"You!" Newlands said. "Have you the heart or the courage for that, Jimmy? And the girl?"

"Tut!" Munroe smiled, waving the thought gracefully aside. "Forget the girl. It'll be an experience for her, that's all. Won't spoil her. It's a question of have to now, Billy. Forget the deep eyes . . . they'll get shallow soon enough without you. Think of the game, Newlands. If we're caught in this, it means a long term for both of us. If we get by with it, it means clover. We've got to fight against the girl, public sentiment, and the police. There couldn't be a harder game or a better one, Newlands."

He knew that he had struck the right note there, and with his usual skill he had left the greatest temptation to the last. Once Newlands felt that he had to fight against two-thirds of the world to put a game through, Munroe knew he would forget conscience and everything else for the excitement of the plan. Five minutes later they were deep in the details of the plan.

Newlands was halfway through supper with Beatrice that night before he ventured the subject. He told her that he had found an old friend who had a house in the downtown district and would be glad to take her in for a time, at least. She was delighted at the prospect of moving into a home-like atmosphere. He talked to her lightly about *Madame* Fenwick and some of her peculiarities, for he feared that this open-eyed girl might notice something strange even in the careful atmosphere of *Madame* Fenwick's. Afterward, he led her to talk of her life, and she ran through short and whimsical annals that kept him between smiles and downright laughter. When she came to the last days of her father, her eyes sought his with a curious wistfulness that made him cold inside.

"Yes, yes," he said softly. "I understand."

"When he died," she said, as if she were determined to have the subject done with once and for all, "I felt as if half my world had vanished."

He nodded his sympathy and thanked God mentally that she was not the whimpering sort. In the meantime, she went on to tell him how they two had played, and read, and talked together all her life.

"He was such a gentle man, Mister Newlands, and such a strong, clean man, too," she concluded. "I imagine you are a great deal like him, but I know so little about men." She smiled apologetically. "Except Dad, of course."

"Except your father, of course," Newlands said, and then he drew her away from her past as skillfully as he had taken her there. He had learned what he wanted to know. Not entirely all, however, for when at the end of the supper he offered her a glass of the same brandy that he drank, and she refused, he was rather piqued. She explained that just a bit of it made her head swim, and that she hated to be confused.

"But it's very pleasant." He frowned.

"I guess it is," she answered slowly, "but I don't like it. That is where my education falls down, you see. Father drank once in a while. I don't think that even he was strong enough for it."

Newlands said no more, but he decided that her education had, indeed, been incomplete. He looked forward with a certain sinister anticipation to completing that education.

Afterward, he sent his chauffeur to Avery's to remove Beatrice's belongings and give up the apartment, while he and the girl took a taxicab to Madame Fenwick's. A servant opened the door to them and smiled faintly in recognition as she saw Newlands. They walked into a private parlor in which a faint aroma of rare perfume still lingered. Newlands ground his teeth. It seemed to him that he remembered that perfume. When Madame Fenwick entered, he thanked his stars briefly but fervently that she was different from the type of her class of women. A single glance from him gave her the cue, and she greeted him with a formal friendliness that would have puzzled the most experienced hostess in San Francisco.

"This is Miss Crittenden," he said, "of whom I sent word to you. I hope you will be able to accommodate her . . . with the best."

There was a faint accent on the last words, and *Madame* Fenwick flashed him a glance of understanding.

"Of course," she said. "I think I have a couple of rooms which will just suit Miss Crittenden. Shall we go up and look at them . . . my dear?"

She hesitated the merest trifle over the last two words, and Newlands saw Beatrice's brows raise a trifle. He shook his head to caution *Madame* Fenwick, and again she received the hint with imperturbable calm.

They examined the rooms together, and, if they were not so large and light as the apartment that she had left, still Beatrice seemed infinitely pleased by their cozy and home-like atmosphere. She smiled her satisfaction mutely to Newlands, but when *Madame* Fenwick left the room, she crossed the room and took him by both hands.

"You have been so dear to me," she said a little breath-lessly, "and today you have almost made me . . . forget . . . forget something which I must not think of any longer." She moved a trifle back, so that she could look into his face more closely. "My father told me," she went on in the low, vibrant voice, "that Fighting Joe Newlands could not have a son who was not a man, and I know that he is right . . . you are such a real man, Mister Newlands, and, oh, I'm so happy to trust everything to your hands."

Chapter Three

CONSCIENCE AND A MIRROR

When Newlands reached his room, he stood for a long time before the mirror. Of all our acquaintances the face in the mirror is the only trustworthy adviser. He has that disquieting habit of saying what he thinks and thinking what he says, a very Diogenes whose lantern lights up the comfortably shadowed corners of our conscience. He repays without the slightest exaggeration our smiles and our laughter, our frowns and our tears. He will not flatter. He cannot cajole. We reckon our minutes by the ticking of a clock, but the face in the mirror gives us the large and pitiless measure of the years. So William Newlands came to a pause, with his necktie half undone.

"You may leave me, Benedict," he said. "I shall get along without you tonight."

When the servant had left, he raised his head again, hoping, doubting, and fearing that the face in the mirror would not repeat what it said before. But it gave back its blackest scowl with another so malevolent that he started.

The lines about the eyes are due to short sleeping hours, thought Newlands.

Debauchery, responded the face in the mirror with a frown.

The widening of the nostrils, he argued, *is . . . is. . . .*

27

The mark of the beast, the face in the mirror shot back, *the sign of gross sensuality.*

And the flabbiness around the chin is . . . is God knows what . . . perhaps a lack of training.

Gratified passions, answered the face.

"I'm only thirty," muttered Newlands, "barely thirty, but how far I have gone. Well, it's been pretty pleasant."

Aye, it's a pleasant way, sneered the face in the mirror, *and it leads to a happy end. Remember Dicky Watson at thirty-eight. Poor Dicky!*

"Bah," said Newlands. "Watson was a weakling!"

What made him weak? scoffed the image.

Newlands passed a hand over his forehead. "I've gone pretty far," he continued. "My God, I never dreamed I had gone this far. But she lied! That's it. She lied!"

What a driveling coward you are, the face in the mirror pointed out almost compassionately. *You are afraid to admit the truth even to yourself.*

"I will change!" Newlands insisted aloud. "I surely can change!"

Too late, the face in the mirror assured him.

"I will never see Beatrice again," declared Newlands. "She was sent to me in an inherited trust. No man would be dog enough to betray her. Why not marry? Yes, why not in earnest?"

Ha, ha, ha! laughed the face in the mirror. *You marry her! You? You tie yourself to the skirts of a woman? Would she be happier tied to you for life? Or you? Bachelor Billy Newlands married? Ha, ha, ha!*

"I'll never see her again," groaned Newlands. "I . . . I'll write to her tomorrow and tell her that I have to go out of town. I'll send her to a respectable lawyer. I'll give her letters of introduction to the best hostesses in town. Yes, by God, I shall!"

Look me in the eye! ordered the face in the mirror.

"So help me, I'll do it!" he cried, and whirled with his back to escape the mirror. "I'll start changing tonight."

It seemed to him, as the thought came through his mind, that the picture of Beatrice flickered into living color upon the wall on the opposite side of the room. He saw again the deep, clear eyes that fascinated him like the changing deeps of water. He heard again the low voice with the peculiar vibrant throatiness. He watched the grave smile and the upward glance beneath puckered eyebrows. Then he turned suddenly back to the mirror, feeling his strength.

Too late! the face in the mirror repeated. *Too late, too late!*

William Newlands flung himself on his bed and buried his face in his arms.

He awoke the next morning to the measured voice of Benedict repeating his name.

"Mister Munroe to see you, sir," said the valet.

"Bah!" Newlands scowled. "What does he want here at this time of the day?"

"Do you wish to see Mister Munroe," said Benedict, "or are you not probably somewhat indisposed this morning?"

Now, as Newlands lay in bed he could look into the long mirror, and in this he could see the reflection of Benedict, although the latter stood beyond his range of vision. As he spoke, Newlands started a little in his bed, for the servant's face was contracted into an ominous scowl. He raised himself a little upon his elbows to make sure, but when he looked at Benedict, the latter presented the same motionless face to which he had been accustomed through ten years. Newlands studied him gravely. He had never been able to penetrate into the emotions of this man, and at the hint that he had seen in the mirror he was deeply moved.

"I'm not indisposed, Benedict," he said, "but bring me a drink of brandy, and I'll be a lot better disposed."

He drank the first glass of the oily fire that Benedict poured him, and looked longingly at the bottle that the valet held tilted above the glass for the second, and then he remembered Beatrice and the subject of liquor from the night before, and shook his head. It seemed to him that he could see a slight brightening of Benedict's face as he refused the second drink, and the valet put back the bottle.

"Show in Munroe," he ordered, and, watching from the corner of his eye once more, he caught a momentary darkening of Benedict's thin face, and he lay back on the pillows to think it over as Munroe entered. As usual, no greeting passed between the two. Newlands never pretended to be cordial with the gambler, and Munroe knew that, excellent actor as he was, he could not hope to be more than a necessary evil to Newlands.

"The Lord be with thee, my son," he began, to show that he was already letter-perfect in his part, "and keep thee out of the temptations which entice the feet of the youth of our nation. In other words, is Beatrice now under the matronly eye of *Madame* Fenwick?"

Newlands glared at him. "The game's up, Jimmy," he said slowly. "I'm through. All through. I haven't the heart to go through with this deal. Never did enjoy playing with marked cards, and this thing is too rank. It's not even a gamble."

"Tut tut," Munroe said airily. "This is a case of conscience and a morning after, Billy. Too late, my son. If you want to be Snow White, you'll have to start far back in your past and use the whitewash brush. How far back, Billy? No, no, too late."

He broke off and studied Newlands, who lay with one hand thrown across his eyes, and above the edge of the hand

Munroe could see the frown.

"I took her to *Madame* Fenwick's, all right," said Newlands, "but I'm going no further. Today I'll take her away and send her back to Avery's. I'll make some explanation to her. Then I'll introduce her to some of the best people I know and let her work out her own salvation. She's too fine to be thrown away, Munroe."

"What does this mean?" Munroe asked slowly, feeling his share of the prospective spoil slipping away from his hands. "Are you going to marry her, Newlands? A real marriage?"

"Why not?" Newlands responded, suddenly uncovering his eyes. "Why not? She trusts me now. She'll come to care for me in time!"

Munroe sneered. "You're in your dotage," he said. "Do you mean to say you'd marry her after taking her to *Madame* Fenwick's? Don't you see that sooner or later she's bound to find out what sort of a place that is, and then, marriage or no marriage, it will be too late for explanations? No, Newlands, it's too late to step back now. You've committed yourself beyond repair by taking her there. You'll have to go through with it even if she is a saint ten times over."

Newlands stared at the ceiling and made no answer.

"The fake marriage is the one way," went on Munroe rapidly. "Get her and get her quick, and, when the money is in your hands . . . why, there are a hundred ways of consoling her after she finds out the fake. Easy, my son. Leave it to me. Besides, as a minister of the Gospel I'm better than Horace Greeley and Billy Sunday put together."

"Get out, Munroe," Newlands stated, dragging his pajama collar open as if it strangled him. "Get out before I throw you out. I mean it!"

It was very evident that he did, and still Munroe hesitated. Caution overcame anxiety at last, however, and yet he paused at the door for a parting shot.

"Think hard and fast, Billy," he said. "Think how far you've gone already. Far enough to queer yourself with the girl in time. Not far enough to do yourself any good in any way. Remember the Edgerleys and the board of directors. Don't act on impulse, Newlands, it's a bad way . . . the worst."

He flung the door open and then started back somewhat. Benedict stood in the door, eyeing him with an impassive face.

"Your mail, sir," said Benedict, as he entered, but Newlands, watching closely, saw a strange glimmer of malevolence in his servant's eye as he followed Munroe through the door with a side glance.

But he spent little time on this puzzle. He was full of the thought that he should go to *Madame* Fenwick's at once and get Beatrice, although he was puzzled as to whether this determination came from a desire to befriend her, or simply to be with her. Then he laughed, hoping to drive the thought out of his mind. After breakfast he went to *Madame* Fenwick's.

"Is she up?" *Madame* Fenwick mumbled, rubbing her eyes and peering sleepily at him. "Of course, she's up and had breakfast long ago. And now she's up and about her room."

Madame Fenwick walked to the hall door and threw it open. "Listen," she said, and turned her head with a rapt smile.

Faintly down the hall came a full contralto voice singing a German song that Newlands had never heard.

"Billy," she said, "you'll have to fight for her with both hands to hold her. She has the voice and the smile that drive men mad, my dear. And when she becomes what you'll make her, she will drive them mad. But, oh, the pity of it, Billy, the pity of it."

"No pity at all," he growled. "You didn't think I was going to leave her here, did you? Bah! I'm going to take her away today. Tell her that I'm here, will you?"

Madame Fenwick walked to him suddenly and caught him by the arm with both hands. "Have you got it in you?" she said in a low savage voice. "Have you really got it in you, Billy Newlands? There are enough of us in the world without dragging in one more, dearie." She threw his arm away from her with a quick disgust. "You haven't the courage. Your blood will turn to fire when you look at her freshness this morning. That's why you're here. There's so much beast in you men that you don't know yourselves . . . you can only suspect how rotten you are. Forgive me, dearie, I'm . . . I'm a little off-color this morning. Of course, I don't mean this at all." She stopped, put her hand on the doorknob, and laughed shortly. "After all," she continued, "I'm going up to send her down to you. You may decide to go down that hall, run down the outside steps, jump into your car, and drive out of this little girl's life, eh, Billy? It would be such a wonderful thing to do, my dear."

He heard the door close behind her, and then he stood with his hands clutched behind him, thinking so fiercely that the words were almost audible on his lips. He felt that he had made up his mind at last. He would not do as *Madame* Fenwick suggested. That was just a little too hard, too brutal, too sudden. No, there was another way.

I will meet her eyes with . . . with a grave smile, he rehearsed in his mind. *I will say . . . "Beatrice, better pack up your things and come along with me. I have another friend who can make you more comfortable."* Yes, that was it. He would take her to Mrs. Alexander Jessup. She would be a true mother to her, bring her out in the best set. . . .

He heard a step coming down the hall. Would she look the

same way this morning? Would her eyes be reddish? Would her voice be hoarse? His heart commenced to pound loudly. The door opened, and he turned with a start.

"Good morning," she was saying. "I'm so very, very glad to see you again, Mister Newlands. All night I dreamed about our lovely evening, and now you're here to show me that the dream was real."

"Good morning," he muttered, meeting her eye with some difficulty. "Beatrice, better. . . ." His voice stuck. He could not speak until he had cleared his throat. "Better get ready for a little trip today," he tried again. "There are still a lot of things to see in this old town."

The Rubicon was crossed at last. If it gave him a pang for the moment, he forgot it the next moment. And he forgot it for a good many consecutive days, thereafter. He was with her constantly. At *Madame* Fenwick's, of course, there was no interruption, and, when they went out together, he scrupulously chose places where his friends would not be present. Once or twice he came close to having to introduce her, but on each occasion managed to dodge the issue, although once it involved bribing a waiter.

He saw very early that he could not win by stirring her to passion. Passion she undoubtedly had, but of a sort that he could never hope to rouse while his own purpose was hypocritical. Sometimes the fact infuriated him, for he knew that he could never take both body and soul in his arms at the same time. He knew that he should never witness in her that terrible and beautiful moment of a woman's complete surrender. But as he watched her from day to day, as the habit of thinking of her grew a part of him, as the sound of her voice and the contour of her face became living reproductions in his inmost self, he knew that, if he could not possess her entirely, he would still never be satisfied until he had gained the one thing he could possess. And after? When he came to this point, he shrugged his shoulders and frowned. Only fools thought of the future.

He was not at all sure that he could win even that part of her, but he had seen women give themselves for manifold and petty reasons. He had seen them go down in a fit of silly and unreasoning jealousy, or in a moment of moodiness and careless despair, and most of all through friendship that they ignorantly thought to be love, and for gratitude.

Those were his touchstones, friendship and gratitude, and he worked toward them persistently with the patience and skill of an acute mind and a great desire. At last the afternoon came when the suspense was too great for even his strength, and, as they sat in her room at *Madame* Fenwick's, he stood in front of her, and in his part of the friend he braced his shoulders stiffly, assumed a controlling voice, hard with emotion, and told her that he loved her.

She started up from her chair with an expression of surprise that was almost terror, and then this changed as swiftly into pity. If he had been a less skillful actor, he would have taken her in his arms then and attempted to sway her with a passionate outburst, but, although the blood leaped dizzily in his brain, he held himself in check.

"I have never loved a woman before," he lied coolly, keeping his eyes steadily upon hers with a tremendous effort. "I never knew that I could feel this way about any woman. But I know now that I can never be happy without you . . . that you are a necessity to me."

He stopped and turned away to the window, and, when he faced her again, his head was bent as though to hide the working of his face.

"You have grown into my thoughts until I cannot think without thinking of you," he went on. "I cannot hear a woman's voice without remembering your voice. The moment you go from me, I am waiting for you, waiting through how many desperately long hours. And to think of a life without you . . . to think of a life during which you may be claimed by some other man. . . ." He broke off shortly and waved his hand as if in despair. "Not that I have a great hope," he said, "but I can't be silent any longer."

He had talked steadily on, knowing that it was best to wait for her first stir of revulsion to die away and to let pity, gratitude begin their subtle work. Now he waited. Yet he could hardly give credence to his senses when she walked to him and laid her hands upon his shoulders, looking gravely into his eyes. He braced himself as if to a physical shock and held that gaze through a strenuous moment.

"I like you a great deal," she said deliberately. "You have been very tender and . . . and very dear to me. It would break my heart to give you pain."

He knew it was the great moment, and, like the great gambler he was, he rose to the occasion without a flutter.

"Dearest," he said in the fiercely controlled voice that was not all assumed, "God never made a man love a woman as I love you. But if you do not love me in return . . . there is nothing I can ask. Nothing!"

She stepped back from him with that little indrawn breath which he knew so well.

"It is so hard!" she cried. "I do so want to do the right thing. I can't tell. I think it must be right to give myself to you if you need me. It is not much to give. I am only a girl, and you are a strong man. I thought love was different, but I do know that I love you with all my heart, and that it would make me happy to please you. So if you want me, you shall have me. Have I done right?"

He took her in his arms, but even then the master actor

knew that he must wait. The arms around her trembled, to be sure, but their pressure was gentle. He touched her forehead with his kiss. It was very well done, for it was not entirely acting, but when he stood outside her door a moment later, he heard a sound as she threw herself on her bed, and then a muffled sobbing.

Newlands swore softly as he started from the house.

But now that he had taken the next to the last step, he shrugged his shoulders at remorse. His first act that night was to ring up Munroe and tell him that the thing was done.

The voice at the other end of the wire laughed sardonically.

"Alas," Munroe said in his most ministerial voice. "Is it even as I feared? Hast thou wandered into the paths of temptation? Leave it to me, chief. Want to see me tonight? I'll be right out."

"No, you won't," growled Newlands. "I don't want to see you till the morning of the . . . the wedding. Good bye."

"Wait a minute!" called Munroe. "Don't be so glum, man. This isn't sure death. It's the short cut to easy street."

"Munroe," said Newlands slowly, "when you go to hell, they'll have to make a bed in order to fit all of you."

Chapter Four

"WHOM GOD HATH JOINED. . . ."

Up to this point Munroe had been the motive force that had kept Newlands working toward the fake marriage, but now every evil in the latter's nature was loosed. He still felt that if he had met Beatrice under ordinary circumstances, she might have come to love him truly, but the very cruelty of his purpose he knew prevented him from treating her with the requisite sincerity. The result was that the more he despaired of winning her love, the more he set his mind upon possessing her body, and this again reacted to rouse all animal passions in him.

The aversion that Beatrice had expressed toward liquor during his first supper with her had stayed in Newlands's mind, and during the period of his courtship, with one or two slight lapses, he had refrained as carefully as a Y.M.C.A. under-secretary. But the strain told on him surely. He could see it himself in his tremulous hands and in the shiftiness of his eyes.

With her customary lack of ordinary excuses she submitted to an early marriage, to an almost immediate marriage, but she insisted that the ceremony take place in the morning.

"Because," she said, "we are beginning everything so brand new, Billy, that we really should start with the start of the day, shouldn't we?"

He thought it strange, but he agreed without much demur. He suggested a very private wedding, and was again delighted to find her pliable.

Through Munroe he obtained a marriage license that was so exact a forgery that it would have baffled the license clerk himself, and through him, also, he purchased a plain gold wedding ring. The ceremony was to lack none of the ordinary frills. They arranged to be married in the little private parlor at *Madame* Fenwick's, and after the wedding breakfast they would take a train for the Sierras. It was Newlands's plan to take her to an obscure resort among the mountains for their honeymoon. After that he had no plans. He never had been in the habit of planning far ahead.

He had to get up perilously near dawn on the morning of the wedding. The sky was blanketed with a dismal San Francisco fog, a wetter and a thicker fog than London could ever boast even on a Monday morning. Newlands went shivering to his bath and came shivering from it. Even the rubdown had not restored the circulation to his body, and, when he dressed, he stood for a moment frowning at his blue and tremulous hand. It flashed into his mind that he could kill an alcoholic breath with charcoal tablets. Under the relief that this inspiration brought to him, he sat down and swore. Then he went to the closet and produced a bottle of brandy. It slipped down with a fragrance that warmed his soul, and perhaps because of that fragrance it lingered at his lips a little longer then it should have. He ate a tablet after that, completed his toilet, and prepared to leave the room.

But a glance through the misted windows chilled his courage. He examined the bottle of brandy again with a somewhat painful curiosity, and then tilted it slowly to his lips.

When he finally left the house, his hands were steady and his step had its old-time spring. He felt fit, amazingly fit. He had not had this nervous elation since the evening on which he knocked out Kid Farwell. He had his auto stop at Munroe's house on the way down, and, when he saw a prim, stiff-backed gentleman with sad mustache walk down the front steps, he laughed aloud.

"Jimmy," he crowed, slapping his friend on the shoulder, "you're the cock of the walk, the kingpinner of them all, the finest thing out of jail!"

Munroe looked at him with obvious concern after this amazing outbreak of familiarity. "Buck up, old man," he said, "what in the name of God have you been doing?" He leaned forward to examine Newlands more carefully. "Yes," he groaned, after a long look, "you've done it! Newlands, what a prize, what a blue-ribbon ass you are. Good God, man, you'd think this was a real wedding, and that you didn't have to have your wits about you. Newlands, you're half drunk already. Are you crazy to do this on this day? By the Lord, I'm half ready to throw up the whole thing now."

"Tut, tut," answered Newlands. "I merely remembered an old recipe for killing the breath. Get cheerful, Jimmy. You're only an hour away from twenty-five thousand dollars. All you have to do is to keep your face, but be careful not to overact the part. She's a close-eyed little devil!"

"And may I be permitted to ask what Benedict is doing on the front seat with the chauffeur?" asked Munroe.

"Sure," answered Newlands. "I've got to have a witness, haven't I? Benedict is the guy."

"I don't like that fellow Benedict," said Munroe slowly. "He has a queer eye."

"Of course, he has," Newlands said, grinning, "when he looks at you. He's not in love with you, Jimmy, but he's the only man in the world who would go to hell for me with a smile. I like him, and he'll do for this job. Don't worry about him. The thing for you to do is to think of your own little job."

"Don't advise me," snapped Munroe as the car stopped in front of *Madame* Fenwick's. "Watch your step, pal. I've started this thing, and I guess that I'm game to go through with it."

Beatrice rose to greet them as they entered the parlor, and with the flush of excitement on her face Newlands thought he had never seen her lovelier. She greeted "Dr. Peabody" with such a gracious and rather tremulous smile that for a moment Newlands feared for the facial control of his collaborator, but he rose to the occasion with the solemnity of a Wilsonian peace note.

"My dear," Munroe said in a profound voice, patting her lightly on the shoulder, "may you be as happy in this union as I am sure God meant you to be."

But when, for a moment, she turned to Newlands, Munroe rolled his eyes significantly heavenward.

The task of introducing Benedict as the witness was strangely difficult to Newlands. When he had mentioned a wife, the man's face had lighted, but when he explained just what sort of a wife she would be, he had gone blank again. His "Yes, sir." and "No, sir." had taken on their accustomed deadness, and it seemed to Newlands that a grave sorrow came into his eyes.

He had shrugged this thought away from his consciousness, yet as he introduced Beatrice to—"My friend, Mister Benedict."—he felt a sudden pang of conscience as the valet, after his bow of acknowledgment, turned to him with dull, expressionless eyes.

Even Munroe showed weakness before he began the ceremony, and Newlands, in an agony of suspense, watched him waste time arranging on his nose a pair of glasses of which he had not the slightest need—he who could read a marked card ten feet away. But once he opened the book and joined their hands, he straightened into his part like a Thoroughbred taking its stride on the backstretch.

Newlands's voice was somewhat overloud and strained, but Beatrice's responses were singularly calm and level. When Munroe came to the phrase—"Whom God hath joined. . . ."—he choked suddenly, and Newlands's heart stood still, but, after a little cough, the deep solemnity of his voice went on the end.

Newlands turned and raised her face a little with his hand under her chin.

"Whom God hath joined?" he muttered, staring into her face intently. "Well, the man isn't made who can put us asunder."

"Of course, there isn't any such man," she said, smiling somewhat wanly up to him. "I'm going to get my traveling bag now, if you'll let me go, and then we go off somewhere and get a perfectly huge breakfast, hmm?"

When she left the room, Newlands dropped into a chair and covered his face with his hands.

"Bah!" cried Munroe. "Don't overdo the part, Billy. I'm willing to admit that you're a wonderful actor, but don't keep on after the curtain is down."

Newlands jerked his head up with a frown that changed gradually into a singularly whimsical smile.

"I'm not acting," he said. "I was just thinking what a funny god has just joined us two. I reckon you're the amateur god, eh, Jimmy? How hell must be laughing now."

He broke into hysterical laughter that sent a shiver through Munroe.

"Come, come," Munroe said impatiently, "you're acting like a child. You're not in a girl's seminary. Brace up. Do you want me to take breakfast with you in order to keep things rolling until the train leaves?"

Newlands shuddered violently. "You are a devil,

Munroe," he said. "Neither blood nor soul in you, but something that isn't red running in your veins."

A sudden passion seemed to change Munroe. He went close to Newlands and leaned over him, talking within an inch of his face. "There's a time coming when I shall sit and look at her through a longer time than a breakfast, Billy," he whispered. "When you're all through with her, I reckon she'll still be good enough for an amateur god, eh?"

He turned and half ran from the house, and the soft-footed Benedict followed him.

Now that the thing was done, Newlands committed himself to the results and found them sweet. He stepped out into the hall, and, when Beatrice ran down the steps smiling to him, he caught her and held her a moment at arm's length, his plundering eyes traveling slowly over her figure until she blushed crimson. Then he drew her closer, pushed back her head with a strong hand, and kissed her hotly, lips, throat, and chin.

He kissed her again and let her go suddenly. She half reeled a step away from him and hid her face in her thrown-up arm for a moment. It was almost as if she had raised the arm to guard against him, and the thought of possible resistance half angered and wholly excited him. He seized the arm and drew it down from her face with resistless fingers, but the curious calculation in her eyes changed his purpose.

"You are very strange this morning," she said coldly. "I have never seen you this way before. It is almost as if I were looking at a different man, Billy."

She stepped closer to him, and under her scrutiny he shrank, and yet he hated himself for it.

"Quite a different man," she added, and then laughed as if to encourage herself. "But it's the excitement, of course. And you let yourself go just a trifle too much, that was it, wasn't it, Billy, dear? And now you're forgiven." Here she reached up of her own accord and touched his lips with hers.

Later, when they sat down to the table, he suggested a drink, and she accepted a gin fizz after some hesitancy. He took a brandy, and after his grapefruit he took another. As the breakfast progressed, she commenced to note that she was doing all of the talking, that his comprehension of what she was saying was indicated merely by nods of the head, but that his eyes remained blank.

After the third drink at the table a meaning did come into them, but it was a meaning that made her uneasy and diffident. She knew little about men, and nothing about emotion, but the starting red-tinted eyes under gathering brows, and the glance which began to move slowly over her body as it had done before when he held her on the staircase, made her tremble and blush. It reminded her of the sensation of a dream when one's clothes disappear in a public place one by one. He was, as she had told him after his first outbreak, like another man. She could hardly recognize his face, his lips had set to such straight, hardened lines, the jaw thrusting out below, and a great vein stood clearly defined across his left temple.

He leaned to her to make a remark, and, as he did so, his hand touched her arm and ran down to the wrist with a slow caress that made the flesh even under the cloth creep. At the same time his breath struck against her face, and the fumes nauseated her. For the second time a grim doubt stalked upon her and made her shiver with a more than bodily cold.

She had hardened her eyes to meet his, but both look and voice were now lost upon him. As she watched with hypnotized eyes, she saw his lips curve slowly and strongly into a smile. She rose in real terror. "I am quite through," she said hurriedly, "and . . . and I'm afraid that we'll miss our train if we stay here much longer, Billy . . . dear!"

Chapter Five

THE MAN WITH THE BLUEPRINTS

Even the pressure of his hand upon her arm as he helped her into the train seemed to her almost sinisterly insistent. He sat opposite to her in the car, and, when she forced her eyes to meet his face, it seemed to her that his nostrils quivered into a greater expansion and that his lips had grown thicker. She noted the folding of the loose flesh over the collar with a little shudder of revolt. When he turned his head, the flesh draped against the point of the collar. Something caught her breath, and she dropped her head.

When she looked up again, he was staring at a watch that lay upon his hand.

"Rotten country," he growled, staring briefly out over the lank, brown plains. "Nothing here but dead land and deader people. My God, how slowly the time goes. I'm going out to have . . . a . . . er . . . smoke."

She knew at once that he was going into the dining car to drink, but she felt strangely only a dim relief at the thought that she would be alone with her thoughts for a moment. He was leaning closer, with the stiff-lipped smile that had startled her at the breakfast table. It seemed as if all the mind and soul were numb and dead, and only so many pounds of flesh remained, so much energy of brute instinct.

"Yes, yes!" she said hastily, nerving herself so that she

would not shrink back from him. "Go and amuse yourself, for I have all these magazines, you know."

He rose with his eyes upon her, and, as he passed down the aisle, she felt his eyes like something physical still upon her. When he had gone, she felt warmer and stronger, and now the thoughts came in a flock.

With an almost religious determination she attempted to occupy herself with the magazines, but the deadly "he said, she said," of the typical story drove her relentlessly back upon herself. In the hopelessness of her situation she could not force away the thoughts of the past life, the play hours of the short dress period, the bedtime stories of the grim-faced man who had been both father and mother to her, and then the eternal romance of the awakening physical being, the mysteries of flowering femininity which she had dreamed to keep pure and fresh against that holiest of moments—the inception of love.

She pressed her hand against her eyes as this thought came on her, and she ground her teeth to keep from crying out. It was not that complete despair had yet come to her. Perhaps this condition of Newlands was only a passing phase that would leave him the strong, confident, friendly man whom she had first known. But all the dread brooding of possible maternity assured her that it was more than this. It was not the liquor alone, although she dreaded and feared that, but she felt that the liquor had merely served to tear away a veil from before her eyes and enabled her to see all the sorry deeps of his nature.

In the bitter wisdom of that quiet moment she knew she had never loved him. She knew that love is something that is glad to be blind to faults, an invisible fire of which a good woman is the altar. An insane desire rose in her to spring up and shout aloud: *Wait! All is lost! All is wrong! I cannot be what*

I seem to be! I am not that man's wife!

It seemed to her for a breathless moment that she had cried out, and then reason assured her it had been only a thought. To quiet herself she began to repeat over and over again in her thoughts: *He is my husband. God has given me to him. This is the end. There is no other way. He is my wedded husband. He is my wedded husband.*

But the more she repeated it, the more it seemed to her strange and incredible that this gross-lipped satyr should have a claim upon her, surely never upon her soul, then wherefore on her body?

"God help me," Beatrice whispered half audibly. "I cannot help myself."

She was not religious; she had rarely been inside a church. But in this moment of bitterness the yearning for comfort was more than she could bear, and she repeated the pitiful little prayer of childhood.

> Now I lay me down to sleep,
> I pray the Lord my soul to keep;
> If I should die before I wake. . . .

She broke off with a shudder at the thought of how Newlands would laugh if he could have read her mind at that moment. She sat bolt upright in the seat, and, as she sat up, she saw for the first time a man who sat farther down the car and across the aisle. By shifting a little in her seat she could see him plainly.

If his face had even been remotely similar to the full, handsome features of Newlands, she would probably have dismissed him from her mind as suddenly as he had entered, but he was in every respect the exact opposite, lean, narrow-jawed, keen-eyed, and his hair thin about his forehead.

Over a little folding desk in front of him lay a scattering of blueprints that he pondered deeply, and, as she gazed, she saw him turn his eyes out of the window. She knew that he saw nothing, that some problem was in his mind alone. He held a pencil poised above a blueprint, and she found herself wondering vaguely whether or not he would solve the problem. There was no doubt about it when he turned his face from the window.

His eyes narrowed a little, and the suggestion of a smile altered his mouth. The pencil moved strongly and rapidly over the blueprint, and then he leaned back and raised the paper to study it more carefully. He set it down again, hesitated, and then picked another print out of the pile and knotted his forehead above it. For some reason she felt a little glow of pleasure over his triumph and a strange surety that he would solve the next difficulty as well.

As she stared at him, it occurred to her that this man was living absolutely shut in by the world of his work in which he wrought calmly, steadily, and surely. It gave her a new sensation of loneliness to look on him so fully employed. She knew that she would not understand what he was doing, and yet she felt an almost childishly strong desire to stand at his shoulder and watch the moving pencil make the little lines which were, perhaps, to alter the labors of hundreds of men. The very silence of such a man had more meaning than the finest eloquence of others.

As the train pulled out from a small station, a telegram was brought him. He ripped it open and read with an emotionless face, and then he raised his eyes. She thrilled somewhat as he stared directly at her, but then she knew that he did not see her at all. His mind was filled by some new thought that left no space for women. The telegram crumpled slowly in his hand, and she watched his jaws set hard. His was the fighting type as well as the thoughtful, not the fighter through physical brawn, but agile, relentless, terrible in action, unconquerable in spirit.

A heavy hand fell on her shoulder, and only by a great effort could she control an exclamation as she looked up and saw Newlands, standing above her. He was long past the stage of red-faced drunkenness, and his eyes glared at her from blue-black hollows. It was typical of the man that he had never seemed so handsome, but the intelligence was quite gone from his gaze when he sat down opposite her. His voice had grown somewhat hoarse, and he talked with the careful syllables of the consciously drunken man.

"Sorry to leave you so long, m'dear," he said, leaning forward to leer at her, rather than smile. "Been awful lonely? Any naughty drummers tried to talk to you while I was gone?"

Unconsciously her eyes roved past him and found the cool, thoughtful face of the man above the blueprints. He was struggling hard with some obviously knotty problem now, but the determination of his face was redoubled, and a certain suggestion of confident power that thrilled her. She looked back to the white, reckless face before her. She had never heard him refer to any business. She doubted if he had ever had anything to occupy his mind. And the doubt no sooner came than she began to wonder if he had the mind to solve any real problem, such as that steady-eyed man down the aisle was now undertaking.

Even in his drunken state Newlands noticed her absentmindedness, and he scowled at her.

"I'm going down the aisle," he said. "You don't seem to feel like talking today, honey, eh? Well, I do. I'm goin' to fin' someone who'll talk."

He half reeled out of the seat and turned to start down the aisle. In spite of herself she could not help but admire the way he pulled himself together and made his legs walk true to the mark. And then she saw that he had fixed his attention upon the man over the blueprints. She noted it with a queer curiosity. She was eager to see the two, face to face.

She saw Newlands bowing profoundly and asking if he might sit down. The other man gathered his blueprints carefully to one side and looked up with an impersonal eye that made her flush. Newlands sat down, and the other merely returned nods and monosyllables. Obviously he was both bored and irritated, but too much of a gentleman to be offensive, even to a drunkard. Again she flushed hotly.

She could not hear their voices over the whine and rattle of the wheels on the rails, and she was glad of it, but she could see that Newlands was growing more and more intimate. Now and then he leaned back in his seat and shook with the loose laughter that had made her shudder before. At last he leaned over and slapped his hand down on the little desk that supported the blueprints.

Some of them went dancing to the floor. The other man leaned over to gather them up. When he straightened in his seat again, she saw that the tolerance had left his face, and the fighting expression sat there.

He leaned forward a little and spoke to Newlands through straight lips. If she had not known Newlands better, she would have thought that he had risen under the fear of a threat. At any rate, he left the seat, paused a moment clumsily in the aisle, and then made his way back to her.

She found then, to her surprise, that she had no care for his progress back to her, and that her only thought was whether or not the man with the blueprints would note that this flabby-lipped drunkard came to her seat. But he had already lost himself upon his papers, and the episode was obviously out of his mind.

The day went too swiftly. The night and the dread of the night were coming on. Luncheon and supper passed in a mechanical endeavor to eat while Newlands ordered more drinks and talked familiarly with the waiters. She was deeply grateful that the man of the blueprints was never in the diner at the same time with them. Sometimes Newlands left her alone for a while in the passenger car to go out for another . . . er . . . a smoke, and each time he was more visibly intoxicated.

And so at last they rose out of the dreary floor of the Sacramento Valley and wound among the foothills that had lain blue and misted along the horizon all through the day. She still thought that she would have another hour of grace left her, when Newlands woke from his half-smiling state of drowsy content and, leaning toward her, said: "It's bedtime, dearie. Better turn in. I'll be along after a while.

She rose without answer. She would have gone anywhere willingly to be free even for a moment from the fumes of his breath and the animal hunger of his eyes, but when she came to the berth, her heart failed her. It seemed to her that, when she had drawn the curtains behind her, she had pulled a veil of sorrow over her soul and shut out hope forever. She drew off her coat with hesitating, dragging movements, and then pulled off her shoes. But here her strength failed her, and she fell back against her pillow weakly.

She lay there for a long time. Now and then a step, passing up or down the aisle, startled her awake with a sudden terror. She opened the window at last to escape from her own thoughts, and looked out upon the calm of the mountains at night, great shouldered forms, all darkly forested, that rolled in solemn procession past her—above them the eternal watching of the stars. She closed the window on the quiet beauty, for it brought home to her a sense of the sordid horror of her own position.

Then she heard the voice of Newlands, thick and almost unrecognizable as he spoke to the porter: "Where's my berth, porter? Where's lower eleven? Thank you, m' frien'. Gimme your arm till I get there. Strange how this ol' boat is rocking. All right, I'm here. Here's a dollar. Goo' night!"

As she heard those changed accents, Beatrice thought of the man of the blueprints during the day. When he had looked out of the window toward these mountains among which they were now passing, he had dreamed of his labors, of his problems, of his conquests. He was the victor, the engineer forever fighting against nature and winning in the end. Those mountains had a significance to him. He would not have closed his window on them. They were like the faces of a strong man's friends to him, his companions, his inspiration. Her thoughts flew back to the face of that lean, thoughtful one she had seen.

The curtains were brushed aside, and the stifling breath of Newlands reached her. She had thought that a rush of energy and revolt would overcome her, but, instead, there was a paralyzing wave of cold, which passed from her feet to her head and accumulated there numbly. She could not speak.

"Here I am, honey," he was saying. "All here. Glad to see me?"

She made no answer. It seemed as if her thoughts were locked from utterance, and she watched him sway weakly away with the pitch of the car.

"Glad to see me, dearie?" he was repeating. " 'Course you are! My God, this car is sure rockin' like a boat, eh?"

A strange commotion checked her reply. The wheels screamed on the rails, the brakes ground loudly, there was a hissing of air lines, and a loud blast on the whistle, and then a crash as if half the world had stopped.

She had seen Newlands reel back into the aisle when the

train commenced to slow down, laughing at his own drunken unsteadiness, but the shock that followed flung her bodily from the berth into the aisle. Luckily she did not strike against any of the uprights, and the tremendous clamor that broke out prevented her fainting from fear. The roar of an explosion followed and shook the car, which had pitched violently at an angle and lay trembling like a living thing. The shrieking of broken air lines and the scream of the exhaust continued, but above all was the crying of human voices in agony.

As she struggled to her feet, she saw the man of the blueprints fighting his way down the confusion of the aisle. But in the dim light she could not see if he was hurt. Then when he was only a few yards from her he relaxed and pitched forward on the floor.

At once a purpose gave her strength. She must get that man out of the car. All thought of Newlands had left her mind after one brief, half-guilty touch of wonder if God had intervened to blot this man out of her life. But here was a man whose life meant something to the world. Him she must save. Already the air of the car was dim with smoke, and she could make out struggling figures here and there in the gloom, but somehow she managed to work her way to the place where he had fallen.

As she reached down to him, her hand touched his naked skin, and she felt it wet with thick, warm blood. The shock, the long horror of the day of expectancy had weakened her, and this last stroke overcame her. She felt the scene whirl before her eyes, and then everything went black.

Chapter Six

A PRISON DOOR OPENS

When Beatrice regained her senses, the air was choking-thick with smoke, and, as she raised her head, she saw that the far end of the car was aflame and long lines of fire licked along the roof of the car. By that light she saw a strange scene of confusion: mattresses and bedding flung into the aisle or hanging out of berths, curtains ripped from the poles, and the windows everywhere shattered. She rose to her knees, and, as she did so, her hand fell upon the warm, wet body of the fallen man.

If her first impulse was to flee, her second was to save this man, this builder and thinker whom she had seen at his work, or to die with him. By the red swaying light of the fire she saw that his back was splotched with blood, but she could see no wounds. The fear came to her that he had already died. He had fallen forward on his face. She bent his face up and back in a frenzy, and, as she did so, the closed eyelids fluttered and the lips parted. There was undoubtedly still life there. The sight of it made her at once happy and desperate, and she felt that if she could save this man to the world, the ruin of her own life would be redeemed.

She glanced behind her toward the nearest door. The way was littered with fallen bedding already smoking with the heat of the fire and from fallen sparks. At any moment the mass of rubbish might become alive with flame. Yet this way lay her only chance of success. If he had possessed the vast muscled bulk of Newlands, she knew that she could not have stirred him, but this man was slighter in build. Perhaps she could manage to carry or drag him to safety.

She passed her arms under his so that her elbows were at the pits of his arms, and lifted his body half erect. It hung on her with a limp and horrible weight. She lowered it again and clenched her teeth over a great sob. In some way she must be able to succeed. She lifted the body again and commenced to drag it back by slow degrees. The entire lower end of the car was aflame before she reached the door with her helpless burden and the fire was swirling rapidly from curtain to curtain. In five minutes more the whole place would be a red hell.

At the door she dropped him again and ran to the bottom of the steps and shrieked for help. She saw a madly confused mob running here and there, lighted garishly by the towering flames of the burning forward coaches. The cries of a hundred voices drowned her own voice to a whisper. She turned back to her task.

To get him down the steps of the car was even more difficult than it had been to drag him on the level, for the nervous strength that the excitement had lent her was passing away, but finally she managed to get him down, half falling and half carried, and then dragged him again painfully until he was a safe number of yards from the car.

Here she dropped the body again, and from her weakness and exhaustion she almost fell with it, but she realized that her work was not yet finished, and that realization kept her senses. She felt now for the first time a stinging pain across the left side of her head, and, when she felt it, her hand came away wet. She could feel a deadly faintness coming on her, and the thought that her strength might fail her before she had made him safe sickened her. She sat by the limp body and threw her head back to wait a moment until her energy returned, grinding her teeth to keep away the encroaching weakness.

Her ears were already half deafened by the outcries she had heard since she had regained consciousness, but sound was not needed to complete the horrors that met her eyes. Men and women ran helplessly here and there crying out and wringing their hands, and sometimes her eyes noted a still figure, even more eloquent of tragedy. She saw three men carry a smoking mass from one of the forward coaches, and she turned her head, sick with horror. Her eyes fell upon a woman crouched close to the ground. In her arms was a little body so limp that a glance showed she caressed the form of life, not the reality.

She raised her glance from the throng and the madness to the dark upper reaches of the mountain with one sentinel pine serene upon the ridge. It seemed as if strength flowed through her as it comes to the devout worshipper through the benediction, and she was able to lean again to her work.

Evidently there was no wound on the back of his body, and with some difficulty, using her knees as a pry and support, she was able to turn him on his back. His arms fell out sideways and his head back with the flicker of the fire red upon his throat. Between wrist and elbow of his left arm was a long gash welling with blood. The faintness came back on her at that. She had never seen a real wound before. But she rallied, calling aloud for help, and set about ripping up her skirt to make bandages. As she worked, she was moaning and talking aloud and unconsciously.

She stopped a moment, under the impression that he had stirred where he lay. Perhaps that was the last pulse of life and the incoming of death! She leaned over and pressed her face against his breast. There was not a stir. She raised her head again and looked at his eyes. They were tightly closed. He could not be dead.

So much horror could not come into her life in one day, or so much vain effort. Again she pressed her face against his breast. This time she felt at last the slow, delayed, and intermittent beat; life was still surely there.

After that she worked with a blind rapidity, muttering and murmuring and sobbing with anxiety. Again and again she cried out for help, but in the uproar her voice was lost. The knowledge that she was left alone to complete her work gave her a desperate strength and enabled her to forget the pain in her head and the sick weakness. Finally the tourniquet was completed. She looked around for something with which to wind it tight, but she found nothing, and every moment might be his last unless that fatal drain of blood was stopped.

She thrust her wrist into the loop of the cloth and moved around and around his body, drawing the tourniquet hard and fast. She stopped when she felt that the bandage had sunk deep into the flesh at the bend of his arm, then darkness came over her at one stride.

It was here that Jack Donnelly and three other men of Steve Crawford's train crew found them—the man lying nearly dead, and the girl unconscious above him with her wrist twisted white in the tourniquet. A little private narrow gauge road ran down from the mine that Crawford's line was working to the main line railroad, and Donnelly had received orders to wait for Crawford when the passenger pulled in that night. But half a mile from Crackens, the name of the station with which Crawford's line was connected, Donnelly and his men saw the big train smash through an open switch. They ran up to find the locomotive vaulted into the ditch of the grading, and the coaches jammed horribly upon it, the baggage car telescoping completely upon the locomotive. During the first few moments they did their share in the work of miscellaneous rescue, but always with an eye out for Crawford. It was Muldoon who saw the woman and the half naked man lying together, and, when he raised Beatrice, he shouted suddenly to the others.

"Hey, boys!" he called. "Here we are, and I think he's done for. Steve Crawford is here under this girl and tied to her. I guess she's dead, too."

They proved to be both alive, however, and after the girl was cut loose from the tourniquet, Donnelly arranged a new bandage on Crawford's arm.

It was obvious enough that he would have bled to death long before if the first tourniquet had not been applied. They decided among them that their obvious duty was to leave the remaining work of rescue to the crowd that had by this time poured out from Crackens, and that their best course was to rush Crawford to the mine on his own train. They could trust the doctor at the mine better than the haphazard physicians of Crackens. They were about to carry off Crawford, when Donnelly, who had been busy arranging a rough bandage around Beatrice's head, was inspired by another idea.

"Wait a minute, boys!" he called. "This here thing ain't all complete yet. We can't carry the boss off and leave his wife, can we?"

"His what?" echoed Muldoon.

"Look at her," declared Donnelly triumphantly. "She was tied to him, wasn't she? Do you reckon a woman would do that for any man who wasn't her husband? Your brains are all turned to muck, Muldoon, if ye can't see that she's his wife. Sure, the boss simply picked up a wife while he was arrangin' his other business down to San Francisco. Never can figure on what these smilin' quiet guys are figurin', can you?"

The condition of Crawford was too serious to stand and argue the matter. Men and women from the little town of Crackens had by this time arrived at the scene of the disaster, and there was obviously no further need of their assistance in the rescue work. Two of the men picked up Crawford, and the others carried Beatrice to the train.

They placed her on an improvised couch in one car and Crawford on a similar one in a second. The girl seemed in no particular danger, so Donnelly left the other three to watch over Crawford. In the meantime, the little train started full speed up the grade for the mine.

It was the whirring of the wheels and the lurch and chuckle of the engine that broke into the mind of Beatrice. It seemed to her that she was walking down many corridors, and every one with horrible blank walls. Door after door she opened, but never the right one, until at last she thought she saw a glimmer of warmer light, flung wide the door, and . . . she looked up into the much-bewhiskered face of Jack Donnelly.

"Madam," said he of the whiskers. "Don't be alarmed, please. You're all right. So is your husband. We found you tied to him with the tourniquet."

"Husband?" she queried faintly.

"Right-o," said Donnelly. "Don't worry about him too much. He may pull through still. He's breathin' steady, and his heart is workin' faint, but sure. I'm Jim Donnelly, ma'am, and one of your husband's oldest men at the mine."

She closed her eyes to think. The whole thing was a muddle. She must still be dreaming. She could hear the rumble of the train beneath her. The wreck came back to her on a rush, and this man said that he had found her lying tied to her husband. She knew now that it must be the man of the blueprints.

"Sure was lucky for Steve Crawford," went on Donnelly, "that you put that tourniquet on his arm. I don't want to alarm you, ma'am, but he wouldn't have had a chance now, if you hadn't. The boys wanted to leave you and Steve up to the mine, but I seen right away that you was his wife. That was why he had the new cabin built up on the hill a month ago. Good old Steve."

He straightened suddenly at the sound of a groan from the next car, and then half ran to the end of the car and into the next. Beatrice sat up, bracing her arms back against the sides of her couch.

Her head still rang, and she felt weak, but, otherwise, she was not ill or feverish. It was the confusion of her thoughts that oppressed her. She knew that she had, in some mysterious manner, come aboard the private train of the man of the blueprints, and there was a vague but tremendous feeling of comfort in that. She had also been assured that the tourniquet had given him a chance for life, and it was this thought that brought her strength back thrillingly.

Donnelly came back to the car followed by three older men. He told her that her husband was better and wished to speak with her. She made no response, but rose and felt her way down the aisle.

In a little looking-glass that fitted into a panel at the end of the car she saw a face that she could not recognize as her own. A great clumsy bandage wound around her head, and over this masses of her hair escaped and fell wildly around her face. Her shirtwaist was half torn from her body and ominously stained everywhere with blood. Another stain passed down her throat where she had fallen across Crawford's body.

She found Crawford lying on an improvised couch much like the one she had occupied, his wounded left arm thrown across his chest and his right arm hanging down toward the floor. As she entered the car, their eyes met silently, and then after a moment she commenced to walk down the aisle toward him. Crawford's face was utterly colorless aside from the great stain across his forehead. The brows contracted heavily, and the lips set in the fighting line that she knew. At the side of his couch she stopped and stared steadily at him. He made an effort to sit up to greet her, but she half smiled and pressed him back with one hand.

"From what Donnelly tells me," he said, and she noted with pleasure that even in that situation there was little save a formal warmth in his voice, "I have to thank you for saving my life with a tourniquet, and, as far as I know, it must have been you who dragged me out of the car. I lost consciousness in there. Did you do that?"

She nodded quietly. The knowledge that she had served this ruler of men gave her a strange feeling of self-possession. Crawford closed his eyes as if to think better, or perhaps from weakness. When they opened again, his glance fixed on her hand. He pointed to the red seared place above her wrist.

"It was you who drew the tourniquet tight?" he asked, still without emotion, and after a little pause, added: "I don't even know your name."

"It is Beatrice . . . Crittenden," she said, flushing slightly, but the name Mrs. Newlands would not come.

"It seems that there has been a ghastly blunder," he went on and, had she not watched him closely, she would have thought that he felt no gratitude for her aid. "My men found you with me unconscious and rather naturally thought that you were my wife, so it seems that they carried you here with me before you recovered. I'm terribly sorry. I'll see that you're brought back to the main line early tomorrow, or whenever you feel fit to travel." As he talked, a feverish color mounted his face.

"And who will take care of you at your mine?" she said.

"I'll make out," he answered, "we have a doctor . . . of a sort."

"A doctor . . . of a sort will not do for you," she declared. "You are weak . . . very weak. Even your voice is tremulous. If you do not receive the best care, this may be serious. You have lost a great deal of blood. Even now, you should not talk."

"It doesn't matter," he said, frowning. "I'll pull through somehow."

"I shall be your nurse," she said suddenly, leaning a little toward him.

He caught his breath at first, but afterward he closed his eyes and shook his head. "I have already compromised you too much," he said. "These fool men brought you here as my wife, and the thing may be difficult for you to explain later. You cannot stay at the camp. You have no idea what a mine is like."

"I don't care," she stated firmly. "I know that you must have care, and good care, from the start."

"It can't be from you," he said. "You have done too much for me already. I'd be unmanly if I let you do this."

She kept her eyes steadily on his. "What would you think of a man who gave up a job he had undertaken before it was completed?" she asked. "Did you ever do that?"

"No," he admitted unwillingly. "But the question here is different. I. . . ."

"There is no longer a question," she said. "I am going with you."

"But," he protested, "you don't know a mining camp. There are no women there. My dear young lady, it is a place where no woman. . . ."

"Even a woman who is known as your wife?" she broke in.

He stared at her with astonished eyes. "You would pose as my wife in order to take care of me?"

"You will be strong enough to take care of yourself before very long, I hope."

"But your reputation. . . ."

She snapped her fingers and then smiled at him and answered very quietly: "Reputations do not weigh against life."

He studied her through a long moment. "I have no right to permit you to do this," he said.

"You are not permitting me," she assured him. "I am forcing myself on your service."

"But your work in the world . . . your position?"

"I am anxious to leave it. I want to leave it all behind me. I want to disappear from the world." She closed her eyes and shivered.

"But your family . . . your brothers and sisters and parents and the rest of them. . . ."

She knew then that she must tell him that she was married. She could not live with and care for this sick man leaving him under a false impression. Yet the thought of Newlands made her sick at heart.

"If I am to go with you and take care of you," she began, "there is one thing you must first understand about me."

"Pleasant or unpleasant?" asked Crawford.

"Unpleasant, I'm afraid."

"I don't want to hear it. I know what you have done for me tonight. If you are going to be with me for a while . . . well, suppose we forget all unpleasantness. If you want me to forget the world you have been living in, why not do so absolutely? The Lord knows you'll have enough chance to do so in these mountains. Shake on it?"

Her hand started to meet his, and then it dropped, and her

head dropped with it. "It is not fair or manly, it is not a just or a manly thing to do," she answered.

"You may be a nurse and a life-saver," he answered, "but you are not a man, you know."

The flush that had been growing on his face indicated a positive fever now. It seemed to her that even while she stood watching him she could mark the shadow growing under his eyes.

"As your nurse at heart," she said, "I order you to sleep and forget everything from now on until you are well."

"But . . . ," he began.

"*S-sh!*" she warned him, and, leaning over, she laid the tips of two fingers lightly on his eyelids.

He seemed disposed to struggle at first and raised his free hand and surrounded her wrist, but he seemed to think better of his determination, and the hand dropped back. The quick sleep of delirium was coming on him as she knew surely it would. His breath began to come quickly and irregularly, and she saw his hand fumbling blindly at the clothes. She slipped hers within the groping fingers. They closed upon it gently. He drew a deep breath, and, as she felt her fingers relax their grasp, a smile grew out on his lips. He was asleep.

She sat alone with her thoughts. The ominous figure of Newlands bulked large upon her imagination. She should have told Crawford that she was married and to whom. What if Newlands discovered her whereabouts and tracked her to the mine to find her living to all appearances as another man's wife? She pressed one hand against her eyes and shuddered. When Crawford awoke, she would surely tell him everything.

But after she had sat there for several long moments, her fingers began working off the golden circle of the wedding ring almost of their own volition. When it finally lay in the hollow of her hand, she sat staring at it, almost without comprehension for a little time, and then, awaking with a sort of shudder, she reached to the open window and tossed the bauble into the night.

Chapter Seven

ANOTHER PORTAL YAWNS

While Beatrice sat by the sleeping figure of Crawford, William Newlands strode blindly through the mountain forest. When the shock of the wreck came, he had been hurled far down the aisle, and the blow, while it left him uninjured, had sobered him sufficiently to make him realize that he must get away from this inferno of pain and sound as soon and as far as possible. He had drunk more that day than he realized, and in the paralyzed condition of his brain he was not able to grasp more than one important idea at a time. Beatrice simply passed from his mind, and he concentrated all of his efforts on getting from the car.

The result was that a moment after the shock he had torn his way through the car, shouldering aside other passengers who were bent on the same object, fought his way through the jammed door, and found himself out in the night. He wanted to get away from this distressing scene, and, as the thought grew fixed in his sluggish brain, his eyes fell on the darkly forested mountainside. Here was a place where he could find cool solitude, shade, and silence. He stepped into the forest with great strides, stumbled into a ravine, and made his way farther and farther away.

By degrees weariness came on him. His mind was still clouded with liquor, and, when he felt like sleeping, he simply searched out a smoothly grassed hillside and lay down. To his estranged thoughts this mad ramble through the dark and into an unknown place had been the most natural thing in the world. Now he slept like a child, with his head pillowed on one upflung arm.

When he awoke, the sun was everywhere on the dew-shining grass and drifted in bright lines through the trees. He heard the burble and run of water, and, looking around, he saw a little freshet trailing through the middle of the hollow. It reminded him that he was mad with thirst.

He went to the stream and drank deeply, crouched on the bank like a great animal. Afterward, he leaned back against the bank to think.

Slowly the last day returned to his mind—the wedding, the drinking, the trip on the train, the sudden horror of the wreck, and, through it all, the face of Beatrice as it had looked up at him, horror-stricken, while he reeled, drunken, in the aisle. He drew himself tensely to his feet and scowled about him with an instinct of defiance, but the truth was beyond his defiance.

He had deserted the woman he had wronged in the moment of danger. Newlands flung an arm across his face and strove to curse, but the sound that came was a groan. He must surely go back to the wreck and find her, perhaps find her dead body, seared with fire and broken.

As the thought came to him, he leaned a little forward over the water. Where he sat, a little in-running of the rivulet made a smooth-surfaced pool astir with pale watercress at the bottom, and now this pool glassed his face. It was the face in the mirror, scowling, intense, powerful with evil. His clothes had been ripped and torn in the wreck and during his wild walk, but the collar and tie were still undamaged, and the hair lay smoothly on his head. In every detail the face that looked up to him was the face that had stared back at him from his mirror, but grosser, he thought, more confirmed in looseness. A bitter revolt came over Newlands.

He knew that he could not go back to the girl and face her now. He would not dare to meet her contempt. If she lived, she would live far better without him. If she were dead—well, perhaps, better be dead than to live with such a man as he, degraded, gross, and brutal, and degrading her always until she had come to his level, or until she had learned the truth of the fraudulent wedding.

With a sudden horror of himself, Newlands ripped off the collar and flung it away, tore open his shirt, and leaned again over the pool. The sight that met him soothed him. It seemed as if he had thrown away ten centuries of civilization with that gesture, and left himself untrammeled of circumstance and ready to fight out a new way through life. A new way! He reared his head up and stared about him.

On either side of the peaks plunged up to the pallor of the sky, all their heights burning in the morning sun, and a rising wind hummed in the forest and carried to his laboring nostrils the fresh scent of evergreens, the eternal incense of the highlands. Here was the place to find such a new way. Here was the place for such a man as he to fight largely and cleanly through to a new life.

He raised his arms above his head and tensed the great muscles slowly with a new consciousness of power. All that past was dead, and rightly dead behind him. It seemed almost as if some divine power had stopped him in the last course of crime before he was soiled beyond all cleansing, as if a hand had reached down and lifted him into this new place, and a voice said: "Begin again!"

Now that all the shadows and cobwebs of circumstance and habit were brushed from his thoughts at a stroke, he saw clearly and judged himself mercilessly, judged the uselessness of all that he had done, knew himself as a mere casual and half-jesting force of destruction.

He saw the meaningless days he had lived; the lean, complacent face of Munroe damned him at every turn. There was nothing to claim him back to that life. Better that he disappear from the old world and become strong in the new. At the thought his blood leaped, tingling.

This was the great adventure, the great gambling chance for which he had always longed. He had never known it, but he saw now that this was the thing, to throw away everything and begin again.

Only one thing pointed upon him like a finger from the past, and that was Beatrice. Yet he knew that the one way he could redeem the wrong he had done her was to eliminate himself from her world. She would learn in time. The fact that he had never been able to make her love him truly was a bitter consolation now. He turned up the ravine and strode on with his thoughts, higher and higher into the heart of the mountains.

Before noon he came upon a little shanty leaning against the side of an upper slope half lost among the trees. As he climbed toward it, he saw half a dozen picks and shovels leaning against the side of the cabin, and a clumsy wooden cradle near them. It was probably a miner's hut, one of those strong-hearted prospectors who venture their luck and determination single-handed to probe the secrets of the rocks and the hills to find gold.

He filled the door with his bulk when he came to it, and, looking in, he saw two men—one frying bacon over an improvised stove and the other washing beans. The keen scent of the frying meat was sweeter than wine to Newlands.

"Howdy, partner?" said the man over the stove, continuing at his task as if it were the most customary event of their lives to receive callers in that wilderness. "Come in an' sit yourself."

The other man said nothing, but raised his head and gave Newlands a sharp look of appraisal as he took his place on a barrel of provisions.

"What might you be doin' in these here parts?" continued the man at the bacon.

"I've been walking to get an appetite . . . and a job," said Newlands.

"Walking to find a job in the mountains . . . in them shoes?" remarked the man with the beans.

Newlands looked down self-consciously at his ten-dollar, low shoes, already bruised and cut on the rocks.

"I reckon we could use another man, though," mused the man at the fire. "What do you think, Mike?"

"Sure we could," answered he who had been addressed as Mike. "Bu. . . ." He broke off, and his eyes ran uneasily over the tattered remnants of Newlands's clothes.

"It's a queer deal, Hen," he added. "Damned queer."

His eyes fastened openly on Newlands as he addressed his partner. Newlands had seen that look before in the ring when he was boxing, but he had never seen such appraisal in ordinary conversation, yet somehow it failed to irritate him.

"Boys," he said, "I suppose you've a right to want to know how I came here, but I'm going to ask you to take a gambling chance on me. You'll find me straight. You'll find me strong." He rose at this point and picked up a sledge-hammer that stood beside the wall, and shook it lightly in one hand. "I may be awkward, but you won't find me afraid of work. If you can use a man, I'll work for my food. I don't want the money . . . yet." He paused, and was rather surprised to see that a dead silence still held the two as they leaned to their tasks. He

70

smiled as he noticed his own omission. "If you want a handle," he said, "you can call me Gilson . . . Jim Gilson." He had had a butler of that name at one time.

The man over the fire turned to him and held out his hand.

"Glad to know you," he said. "I'm Henry Peters, but most of the boys call me Hen and forget the rest of it. This here is Mike Corley. We got a sort of a claim down here that ain't panning out too good just now, but we're stickin' to it because we got hopes. We've got nothin' much but hopes and grub now, and that's why we can't pay for help in the mine. If you want to dig in here till you . . . er . . . get on your feet, why, you're sure welcome to the chow . . . an' we'll pay you back wages if we hit pay dirt. Does that sound good to you?"

"It does," Newlands declared, shaking hands with the men and wondering at the wooden hardness of their hands. "I make only one bargain . . . that you don't ask me any questions about my past. Just forget that I ever lived a day before this one. I'm starting life now. Get me?"

"Sure," broke in Mike Corley, showing his first sign of enthusiasm. "If we ask you any questions, you come right on back an' ask some questions on your own hook. I reckon that'll always stop the music box . . . eh, Hen?"

The three men broke into unanimous laughter. Five minutes later Newlands was swinging an axe to turn a dry log into firewood, and, as he worked, he sang.

Fifteen miles out of reach of his singing, fifteen miles through the heart of the Sierras, was the Victory Mine, and Beatrice at the side of Steven Crawford.

Chapter Eight

WANTED: A DEVIL OF A MAN

Crawford was still delirious when the little train arrived at the mine. It was Donnelly's suggestion that they place him in his old cabin because they would not have to carry him so far. He arranged the place as quickly as possible for the sick man, and then pointed out the new cabin at the top of the hill where he indicated Beatrice should sleep, "because this here place ain't fit for a woman to sleep in, ma'am, an' the new cabin is good enough for a queen, almost."

In the meantime, the physician of the mine appeared. Beatrice asked him what sort of a diet the patient should have, and he replied: "Something light, ma'am . . . gruel an' . . . er . . . mush, an' things like that."

She smiled at the idea of a man nearly dead from loss of blood attempting to regain his strength on gruel and mush. She saw at once that the whole burden of care for Crawford would fall upon her, and she was almost glad of the responsibility. After the doctor left, she made Donnelly undress and wash her patient, while she found some clean bedding. Between them, they made Crawford as comfortable as possible, and then she turned low the kerosene lamp and settled down to the long vigil.

For seventy-two hours she dared not leave the cabin.

During most of the time Crawford was delirious, and the food that she prepared for him she usually had to force into his mouth. At the end of the three days, however, he fell into a natural sleep, and Donnelly half carried her up the hill to the new cabin. There she slept the round of the clock, and woke on a fresh morning with new life and strength.

It was a comfortable little cabin. One large apartment served as both sleeping-room and office. A roughly built desk occupied one corner, with a row of scientific books upon a shelf over it. The bed itself was built solidly against the wall, with curtains arranged so that it could be shut off and the room turned into a business-like place. In the little kitchen that formed the other room was a small range, and an array of iron and tinware more durable than attractive. But the cabin was like a home to her; it was her sphere, the throne from which she overlooked the forested mountaintops.

It had been owing to the consideration of Jack Donnelly that some simple frocks had been brought up on the branch train from the general merchandise store at Crackens, and now she arrayed herself in a fresh dress with no little self-consciousness, for, when Crawford awoke that day, he would undoubtedly be in his right mind, and the instinct to please was strong in her.

When she opened the door that morning, the prospect gave out over a thousand ravines and back to snowy peaks, one out-topping the other until the far-off ranges, blue as mist, lost themselves against the sky. She had never seen such a place. She had hardly dreamed it, living among the little narrow ridges of Oahu, and these jagged piles, like muscularly upthrust arms of nature, thrilled her through. It gave her new heart to go back and fight the fight for the man who lay between life and death in the cabin below. In such a place, how could death conquer a strong man's determination to live? The very air that fluttered the skirts about her as she walked down the hill was chill and keen as the instinct of life.

Donnelly rose with heavily circled eyes as she entered the lower cabin, and nodded to her that Crawford had slept all night. Between them, they agreed in soft voices that Donnelly was to take the night watches, and she would care for him and prepare his food during the days. Then the Irishman left, and she went by the bed.

The shadow of death still lay upon his face, but unquestionably the crisis had passed. His pulse was even, although faint, and his breathing was deep and regular. Yet the pale, thin face testified how far he had walked in the valley. Only with care could she bring him back to the light.

She knew as she looked at him that if it had been Newlands she could never succeed. His was a fierce strength that would have fought death with a convulsion and conquered or died in a moment. But in Crawford she perceived the strength of patience and determination that, in the end, might win out even against odds.

These were the two men she had known in her life. The one she respected, admired, felt perfect confidence in; the other she feared, almost loathed, and yet there was something more than fear or loathing that brought him back so vividly to her memory time after time.

She set about preparing a breakfast for Crawford, for, when he woke, she knew he would be ravenously hungry. She found a box of oranges, and split one in two. Then she boiled some eggs, and fried bacon thin and crisp, and made wafers of toast.

When she came back from the little room that served as a kitchen, she found his eyes open and steadily upon her. The smile that greeted her was eloquent.

"It was the bacon which woke me up," he said. "The

sweetest perfume in the world! Do you know, I feel as if I had been sleeping and dreaming through countless years, but, in the end, I knew I should wake up and see you."

She laughed lightly and sat down by the bed. His hand fell naturally over hers, and yet there was no familiarity in the touch.

"Are you very hungry?"

His smile was eloquent, and she rose and brought in the tray. The tray itself consisted of a piece of rough board, but she had covered it over with a napkin, and the food she covered with another. The eagerness of his face made her laugh as she set the tray down and withdrew the cover. But when he came to eat, it proved a difficult matter. She had to assist him to sit up in bed and prop him with pillows, but even then he had a hard time. His pale fingers had scarcely enough strength to force the spoon into the firm, rich meat of the orange, and the first spoonful he raised with such a shaky hand that all the juice was sprinkled upon the clothes.

He looked at her with eyes of real despair, and she studied him with concern.

"I didn't realize," she said slowly, "of course, you are terribly weak. Now let's try this way."

She took the orange from his hand and dug the spoon into the fruit and raised it to his lips. He crimsoned with mortification, and shook his head.

"Nonsense," she laughed. "Just imagine you're in a hospital, and I'm a trained nurse."

She cajoled him into swallowing the first spoonful, and after that his appetite seconded her arguments with irresistible force. In time he submitted entirely, following the rise and descent of the spoon with his glance and raising his eyes to her face like a child when the spoon touched his lips. It was the absolute dependence of this strong man that unnerved her.

If her first meeting with him had taken place during the wreck, it would not have been so hard for her, but she had seen him at work, absorbed, impersonal, fighting obstructions and conquering them, and now he was as helpless as an infant under her hands. Every woman loves to give herself greatly, and the impulse warmed Beatrice through. With the work of her hands, with the cheer of her presence, with the patience of her labor and tact she was bringing this big constructive force back to the world of living and struggling men.

Yet she knew that she was unjust. He looked upon her as a free woman, and yet she felt herself tied forever to a man whose memory was horror, terror, and fascination at the same time. With Crawford she felt a respect for his intelligence and for his moral force, but the thought of Newlands was the thought of emotions so strong and impetuous that the memory of them touched her half with terror and half with awe.

Perhaps it was the fear that Newlands would come upon traces of her before long and appear suddenly to claim her that impelled her more than even her innate honesty to make a clean breast of all her past to Crawford. She knew that he would be horrified and sympathetic, and she felt, also, that the news would kill forever in him something that, she could not but know, grew from day to day. It looked on her from his eyes. It rested on her with his smile. It pursued her to her cabin at night.

She postponed the day as long as possible. She excused this delay to herself by the fact that Crawford was very ill and that he manifestly should not be troubled with extraneous worries. But finally the day came when the color in his face made her acknowledge with a sinking heart that the time was come. He had asked her if he could not sit up that day, and then she came and stood by the bed, straightening like the soldier who faces a dangerous duty.

"On the night you were hurt," she began, "I started to tell you something, although you have forgotten the incident long ago."

"You started to tell me something unpleasant," he said.

"Yes, it is unpleasant."

"And are you going to tell me now?"

"It is something you ought to know," she said.

"About yourself entirely?"

"Yes," she answered, "it is entirely about me."

"And unpleasant?"

"Yes."

"My dear Beatrice," he said, "there is nothing in the world unpleasant about you that I must know. If you ran away from home because you got tired of teaching school, I assure you that it makes no difference to me and I don't want to hear about it."

"It was much more than that . . . ," she began.

He grew more serious as he saw the real trouble in her face. "Listen to me," he continued. "I only know of you that you saved my life when all the men near me were too much concerned with their interests to lend a hand. I know you helped me when you were badly hurt yourself. I know that you stayed with me and kept me from bleeding to death.

"I know that you came with me to this mine and have even pretended to be my wife so that you could care for me, and that you have worked day and night until at last I am out of the shadow of death. That's all I know, but it seems to me about enough. It's more than I know about any other person in the world."

She had dropped her face between her hands and answered nothing.

"There is something that makes you unhappy," he said

gently. "But I don't want you to call up the ghosts of your past before me. If there are ghosts, why, let them be dead, indeed. I know a clean-hearted, beautiful, brave girl, and I will not have her spoiled by her own extravagant conscience. I know there has never been a real shadow in those eyes, nor an unclean or unworthy thought in your mind."

She dared not face the strong assurance of his eyes, and she looked away from him as she answered. "You are too generous to me," she faltered.

He placed his hands firmly over his ears and closed his eyes, wrinkling his face with comic seriousness. "I will not hear," he declared. "I know only one Beatrice. If you want to introduce another one, go talk to the mountains . . . they can stand it better than I."

In this manner they came to some sort of truce on the matter. Once or twice on the following days she attempted to bring up the subject, but on every occasion he closed his ears against it.

It was he who finally suggested that she might openly tell the men of the mine that she was not his wife, but this was manifestly impossible. There was not another woman in the camp, and an unmarried woman was unsafe there—more than unsafe. As long as she stayed there to nurse him, she must stay as his wife.

This in turn brought another complication, and a far more serious one for the future than any in the present. While Crawford was very ill, it was natural that she should live in the cabin on the hill while he stayed below, but when he began to grow strong, they would have to occupy one house, or the men of the camp would grow suspicious. To be sure, when he grew strong, she could leave the mine, but to leave the mine meant to go back to the world of Newlands and all the terror of that endless day upon the train. No matter which way she turned in her thoughts, she seemed hemmed in with impossibilities.

She was almost glad that his recovery was slow. Had he been undisturbed, nothing could have prevented him getting on his feet within a few days, but troubles from the mine continually poured in to him, and his mind was eternally distraught with the problems for which there seemed no solution. Sometimes Donnelly came up and sat with him through long conferences, and, as she passed in and out of the room, Beatrice gathered the substance of the difficulty.

Crawford held a lease and option of purchase on the Victory Mine for a term that would expire within some thirty days. He was confident that he could discover in the mine a rich lode, but up to the present his men had only struck streaks of temporarily rich pay dirt, not enough to meet the expenses of the big gang. In the meantime, Crawford had interested a rich company that would willingly buy the mine and give him a large interest if he could strike the lode that he was positive lay there. His one chance was to uncover the lode within the period of the lease.

Another difficulty was that he must hold the men closely at the mine. If they went down to Crackens on pay nights, they would be sure to make damaging statements concerning the mine, and these would in turn ruin his chances with the investment company which was already interested in several rival claims. But the necessity of keeping the men close to the mine irked him. They were all free mountaineers, used to rambling about at their will after working hours, and the steady confinement maddened them. They had all signed contracts to work steadily during the period of the lease, but a signature was a small chain upon such men.

The time came when affairs reached a crisis, and the miners sent a delegation to talk with Crawford. From the kitchen where she sat, Beatrice could hear Crawford cajoling, commanding, and pleading with them. Their gruff monosyllables in return indicated that he was having little success. They wanted one day of freedom, and, after that, they would be willing to return and work till the end of the thirty days remaining. Without that day of freedom—there was an eloquent silence around the room.

In vain, Crawford explained that one day of license would be as fatal to his interests as a month. In vain he implored them to remember their contracts. The stolid silence answered him.

Beatrice peeped through the door and looked at the sullen faces of the men, great-shouldered, unshaven fellows, with the grime of the mine still clinging to their boots. Finally, when Crawford was manifestly exhausted, she entered the room and told him that he must talk no longer. The men rose as she entered, and she could see their labor-hollowed eyes burn on her from head to foot. Then they turned and filed out of the room, the little cabin echoing hollowly to their footsteps.

That afternoon Crawford, shaken and feverish as he was after the excitement of the morning, insisted on talking with Donnelly. With Donnelly he outlined a new plan. Several of the most trustworthy men were to ride through the country to all the nearby claims and ask for laborers at the rate of ten dollars a day until the period of the lease expired. With the help of a score or more of new men the work might be pushed rapidly enough, so that the lode, if it was there, would be uncovered. If it was not uncovered soon, the men would certainly break away from him, and then ruin was unavoidable. Donnelly was plainly pessimistic.

"It can't be done, Steve," he growled. "I've tried and tried with the men. I've made 'em promises. I can't do anything more. Yesterday someone shied the end of a timber at me, and it knocked the lantern off my hat. When I turned around, I seen those two swine, the Upton brothers, standin' at the end of the passage pretendin' to be shovelin' as if nothin' had happened. I didn't dare speak to them. I don't dare drive 'em any further. If something happens to rouse 'em, they'll start for it and will kill me first in order to get away."

Crawford raised himself on his elbows. "Donnelly," he said, "you aren't going to show up yellow on me, man. Why, Jack, you know all my plans. You've been with me since the start of this thing. You know that I'm a success or a rotten failure just as this mine turns out. I've staked everything on it. It's my pet dream. If it fails me, I'll be the laughingstock of mining engineers all through the mountains. Jack, you've got to go back and quiet those men."

Donnelly shrugged his shoulders. "What could you do with 'em yourself this mornin'?" he asked sullenly.

"Nothing!" cried Crawford bitterly. "Nothing, damn them. I need a machine-gun to open their thick skulls to a single thought. It needs some other kind of driving power than mine to handle those men. I can't do it. Jack, it's up to you."

Donnelly shook his head slowly and crumbled the soft hat between his hands. "It ain't up to me," he said. "I know when a job's my size, an' this one is cut too big. I can't do it. I'm nearly through. I'll give you what I've got. I may be able to hold 'em for a day or two. But the end is comin' soon. They're beginnin' to form in groups in the bunkhouses at night, and they stop talkin' when I come near 'em. I reckon you know what that means."

Crawford closed his eyes and groaned with anguished helplessness. "Oh, God, Jack," he said at last, "if we had only some man who had more devil in him than all the rest combined we might win out yet. Sometimes the devil wins where a mere man fails. But we've got to take our only chance that's left. Send out half a dozen good men this afternoon to all the nearby claims, get in some new blood that'll keep them quiet for a while. Men from the outside will put them in touch with the world again. These poor devils haven't even seen a paper for weeks. The men will tell them the news. Then tomorrow at lunch hour I'll go down myself. I'll get four men to carry me down, and I'll talk to them and try to drive some sense into their heads. That's all we can do."

It was done. Late that afternoon a rider worked his way up a cañon and came upon the three men working on Henry Peters's claim. Henry and Mike would not leave their claim even for the tempting sum of ten dollars a day, but Jim Gilson was plainly interested.

Chapter Nine

THE DEVIL TAKES COMMAND

The weeks of labor had made a new man of Newlands. The cropped mustache with all its suggestion of refinement he had shaved off, and he had let a short rough beard grow about the lower part of his face. This change, combined with the fact that the sweaty pick-and-shovel work had made his face lean and taken away all suggestion of grossness, made him as different in appearance as if he had worn a mask. His very voice, once fleshy and husky from excessive smoking, was now clear and strong from much deep breathing of the keen mountain air.

He leaned upon the short-handled shovel, a very Hercules of toil, his sleeves rolled halfway up the knotted muscles of his arms, the proudly corded throat open and already tanned by the sun.

"Your talk sounds good to me, my friend," he said to the messenger. "I'll go with you."

"Don't be a fool," broke in Mike anxiously. "It ain't that we hate to lose you, though I admit that I never seen your like for the shovel or the sledge-hammer. But don't go to work for Steve Crawford. He's a crank. It don't pay to work for a freak with a lot of theories."

"As long as he has the ten-dollar bills, I don't mind his theories." Newlands smiled. "I'm going."

Mike and Hen shook hands with him regretfully, and he stalked off down the valley after the horseman, who explained to him on the way the terms under which he was to work. On the whole it appealed to Newlands. His first taste of working in the soil had not been unpleasant. The smashing of the rocks, the constant strain of the shoveling had been a pleasure to him, and he rejoiced, as every strong man rejoices, to feel his muscles grow into a whipcord and agile strength.

The idea of confinement in the mine or bunkhouses of the mine was unpleasant, but not enough to keep him back, and there was something about the unusual nature of the proposition that excited his sporting nature. It seemed to be one man making a hard fight against serious opposition—one man taking the long chance in hope of one great success.

As he sat on the edge of his bunk that night, he heard the various grievances of the men. They admired Crawford, but in a distant way. He was not their type of man, and they knew and resented it. They recognized in him the man to whom the idea is everything and accomplishment is greater than personality. Consequently, in their respect for him was mixed a little fear and some hate, with the latter element evidently growing. They admitted that he had their signatures on contracts such as the one that Newlands had signed that evening, but they claimed that he had no right to inveigle them into such a contract.

"Soft enough for him," stated one black-bearded warrior of the pick when the others had fallen into a brooding silence. "He's lying up there in his cabin with a swell wife to take care of him. Little he cares for us poor devils, without so much as a smell of booze on the lot of us."

"How does he know? He don't even drink! I've served my time in the mines, but I never worked for such a guy, and I'm damned if I'm goin' to work much longer. I'm through. He's got me on a contract, all right, but once I get shut of this outfit, he can hold me to the contract if he can get me. Am I right, boys?"

A solemn chorus of assenting grunts answered him, and then Newlands saw a much bewhiskered man approach them. At once there was a whispered—"S-sh."—around the circle, and, when Donnelly came up to them, not a man spoke. He stood, hesitating for a moment, and then he walked on. The men followed him with eyes of hate.

"There's the spy," said one of them to Newlands. "Look out for that guy, Gilson. He's no good. Stands in with the boss. Gives us a lot of hot-air talk about being faithful. Pah!" He spat violently with disgust.

"I reckon the air's gettin' tolerable unhealthy for him around these parts," volunteered another. "Some of the boys are out to get him. I saw a stone drop down the shaft the other day and land within an inch of his head. You ought to have seen his face when he turned 'round. I couldn't keep from grinnin'. An' he didn't have the guts to say a word."

While they spoke Newlands felt the muscles of his arms involuntarily tensing, but he was too wise to speak. He judged that this crowd was a single unit on one thing—to leave Crawford's employment and let the Victory Mine go to the devil, and his heart went out to the man who lay sick in the cabin that he had passed.

The next morning he went to work with his shift, and, as he worked, he noticed that the men around him were over-leisurely and listless in their actions. They had no heart in what they were doing, and they did not care to hide it. When a boss spoke to them, they made no answer or else cursed covertly.

Newlands watched and waited and noted faces. The ma-

jority, he decided, were simply great unreasoning hulks tha
would not have been discontented had not a few talkativ
ringleaders supplied them with objects of wrath. But he saw
here and there, sharp-faced men who paused frequently
leaning on their picks or shovels, to talk out of the side of thei
mouths to fellow workers. Above the rest he watched on
blond giant, a man far over six feet in height, and built per
fectly in proportion, evidently a fellow of vast strength, an
moving with the ability of a cat in spite of his bulk. Physicall
and mentally he seemed to be far in advance of the re
mainder, and because, perhaps, he felt this double superi
ority, he seemed to feel that it was his duty to be in th
forefront of every movement. Where he spoke, the me
leaned forward to listen, and Newlands noticed with interes
that, when his eye met the eye of a boss, it did not drop o
shift.

At the noon hour the men ate in sullen silence, with the ex
ception of the blond, who Newlands discovered was name
Georgeson. He spoke in a loud voice, taking a boyish glee i
enumerating his grievances against Crawford and watchin
the effect upon the rows of listeners who were not quite bol
enough to say the same things. In this handsome youth New
lands recognized at once the leader of the revolt. What he di
the rest would instinctively imitate.

A disturbance at the door attracted his attention, and h
turned on the bench to see a pale, slender man carried int
the room in a chair that was almost a stretcher. Donnelly
cleared his throat and rose from the table as the four me
placed Crawford down at the end of the room.

"Boys," said Donnelly, "there ain't no doubt that some o
you think that you've got troubles with the boss, and so her
he's come down to talk things over with you, though any ma
of you can see he ought to be back in his bed. Now, any of yo

that has something to say, stand up on your hind feet and talk. He's here to listen."

A deep silence followed the remark. For a moment Newlands thought that the sick man would win the day, and his heart warmed at the bravery of the invalid facing this black-hearted crew in the midst of their discontent. But he had not counted on Georgeson.

The giant rose and spread his great hands on the edge of the table. Evidently he saw here an opportunity to make himself openly what he had long been in secret, the leader of these scores of men, and leadership was too sweet to him to let the chance pass by.

"Sure, we'll speak," he said in a great voice; "and we sure got a lot for Mister Crawford to hear. We been in this here damned hole, slaving for him for weeks, an' we ain't hardly seen the light of the sun. It's got to stop, that's all. We got to have a chance to go down and see the town and lap up a little booze. We need it. Why, my throat is so damned dry I can't hardly talk right now."

A deep chuckle passed from bench to bench at this vital remark.

"An' what difference would one day off make to the work in the mine?" He paused and looked around the table, and every head nodded assent. There was not a question about unanimity of opinion. They were behind him to a man. "We'd simply get out an' get some air," he went on, warming to his subject, "an' then we'd come back an' work like hell till our contracts are up. That's all I got to say now. There's a lot more I could say if I was pressed. That's all."

He sat down amid a rumble of applause. Newlands watched Crawford eagerly, and saw that his face was flushed with anger, but that he was making a hard fight to keep control of himself.

"Boys," began Crawford, and his voice was steady enough as he spoke, "I'm mighty glad to hear what you've had to say. I know that it has been hard to stay in the mine as long as this, but I'm sorry to say that I'll have to hold you to your contracts . . . every one of you."

He paused a moment, and in the pause Newlands knew surely that he was going to go too far. This man was used to technical problems, not to handling or leading men. His heart went out to him.

"When you were employed," continued the engineer, "every one of you was told just what you would have to expect. You were told in detail what your work would be, and under what conditions we would accept you. You agreed to these conditions. I have your names in black and white. What you say about one day off is nonsense. I have strong reasons for wanting present conditions in this mine kept secret, and one day would be enough for all of you to tell everything you know. It's madness. It would ruin all my work and kill my chances. It's my big game here, and I expect you to be men and stand by me. Remember, you have made a legal agreement."

Georgeson rose suddenly in his place. He had perceived the psychological moment. "Agreement be damned!" he roared. "What do a lot of words on a piece of paper mean to a man who wants work? You knew that, and you knew that if we'd understood what you wanted of us, we would never have come. How can a man know what bein' in prison is like until he gets there? I'm askin' you that. Besides"—here he pointed a dramatic finger at Donnelly, who stood by the side of Crawford—"you've got a lot of sneakin' spies hangin' around to listen to what honest miners have got to say, and then go and tell a lot that he never heard to you. You're no good, Jack Donnelly, an' I'm here to tell you so!"

The dramatic force of this statement was so vivid that the lack of logic in the earlier part of it was overlooked. A loud roar of anger rose from the men at the tables. Donnelly turned pale. A braver man than he would have quailed before those rows of hard, fierce faces all turned upon him.

"Boys," he began, "you're all wrong about me . . . I. . . ."

"Shut up!" yelled another voice from the crowd. "Don't try to soft soap us now. We're goin' to get you, Donnelly."

"There's no time as good as now!" called another voice.

The break had come. Already men were rising here and there at the tables. Newlands slipped away from the bench and stole into the background near the end of the room. By the wall he found a sledge-hammer handle that one of the miners had dropped when he entered the mess hall.

"Men, listen to me!" called the voice of Crawford.

"We've had about enough of you, too," said another voice.

"Let's get Donnelly now!" called another, and, accompanying the words, a great tin cup of coffee whirled past Donnelly's head. A score of men, encouraged by this act of violence, crouched to rush the foreman. The time had come. Fearing it was almost too late, Newlands leaped in front of Jack Donnelly, and, as he whirled the oak club over his head, the onrushing crowd split to right and left and cowered back. The sway of those great shoulders told them that this man meant business, and bad business for the first men to come in his reach.

But Newlands's eye was upon Georgeson ten feet away, and crouched like a tiger to leap at the first opening.

"Get back, you fools!" roared Newlands. He could see the men start at the thunder of his voice, and the sight pleased him more than the applause of a crowd. He made the rest of his talk with the club poised lightly over one shoulder like another Gurth standing, the last man under the Saxon standard.

"Are you men or dogs?" went on Newlands. "Do you hunt in packs? Have you any reason or decency in you? Get back there, you with the yellow hair, or I'll brain you as sure as God made little apples! You, too, you black-faced dog! Your head is thick, but this will let light into it."

It was a poor enough joke, but it came at a crucial moment. Moreover, it gave the chance that Newlands wished to give the crowd to back down at the expense of one of their number. Not a man there, he knew, but was ashamed by this time of the fact that they were about to rush one man and an invalid. A dull roll of laughter passed through the crowd.

"One on you, Harry!" called a voice. "The ivory may crack!"

The men laughed again, and there was a general backward movement toward the benches that they had just left. They were beginning to think of their food again.

"Listen to me," went on Newlands, anxious to keep them on the run while he had the upper hand. "We have something to complain of. There's no doubt of that. Crawford is a reasonable man. I know a real man well enough to see that. I'm going up to his cabin with him and talk things over with him. We'll compromise some way, and it'll be better off for all of us."

"Who elected you?" called a voice.

Newlands made a step forward and pointed out the man who had spoken. His other hand tightened upon the handle of the hammer resting on his shoulder.

"I elected myself!" he roared. "You're the skunk who threw that cup a while ago. I saw you."

He hadn't seen him, but he knew that he must make his talk short and strong. He could see the fellow wince. It is one thing to be part of a mob and another to be singled out of it.

"I saw you," repeated Newlands with conviction, "and, if

you open your face again while I'm speaking, I'll bust you in two. Understand that? Also I repeat that I've elected myself to this job. If there's anyone here who wants it more than I do, he can stand out and I'll argue with him."

A chuckle of appreciation answered him. He saw Georgeson start up in his seat and then sink down again. Evidently the big fellow was not afraid, but had not yet quite made up his mind. For the moment he had won the day.

"You boys go back to your work," he went on. "When you come in this evening, I'll have something to tell you, and, if it doesn't suit you, why . . . we'll all leave in a bunch. Does that sound good to you?"

A roar of approval answered him, and he turned to Donnelly, who was leaning forward with a drawn face.

"Get Mister Crawford out of here," said Newlands. "I want to talk with him alone."

They raised the chair, and he followed them from the mess hall into the open air.

Chapter Ten

"IT IS BETTER FOR HER"

They made their way toward the cabin in silence. Donnelly paused a moment to wring Newland's hand, but for the rest nothing was said. Crawford leaned back in his chair, white and exhausted by the scene, until they had placed him in his bed again.

"You fellows can go," he said, "and thank you. Everyone go except you . . . what's your name?"

"Gilson," Newlands said quietly. "My name is Jim Gilson."

Crawford fixed a keen glance on him. "I've got a lot to say to you," he said. "Wait just a moment."

As Crawford spoke, Newlands turned his head to follow the sick man's eyes, and saw a woman carrying a tray. Full of the scene which he had just passed through, Newlands at first saw nothing save the white dress, and decided that she was a trained nurse brought to the mine to take care of the engineer; but as she passed him without a glance, and he saw her face in profile, Newlands shrank and blanched under his tan, for it was Beatrice.

His first impulse was to flee, as the thought of his crime against her came on him. A moment later he knew that he was safe in his disguise with the shaven mustache and the growth of beard. He remained to be torn with emotions.

Very dimly he heard her speaking to Crawford as she uncovered the tray of tea and toast and some fried fish.

"Some trout that Jack Donnelly caught yesterday," she was saying. "I fried it crisp because I know you like it that way. And all in butter. I knew you'd be hungry after your talk with the miners. Tell me how it came out. Could you handle them?"

"They yelled me down," Crawford said bitterly, and Newlands observed that he was taking Beatrice's attentions almost as a matter of course. "They would have mobbed me if it had not been for this man, Jim Gilson."

At this she flashed her eyes toward Newlands, but he knew, and was almost grateful for the knowledge, that she did not see him. Her thoughts were all for the sick man before her.

"This is the man who saved me," continued Crawford. "This is the fellow who stood them off when they were about to make a break for it. My God, it was wonderful! Beatrice, he stood up there before the lot of them when they were raging like a pack of wolves, and challenged them with a sledge-hammer swung over his head." Crawford closed his eyes a moment and drew a deep breath. "I would give ten years of my life to be able to do one thing like that," he said at last.

Newlands, sick at heart, had no eye for him. He only knew that Beatrice stood gazing at him with shining eyes that were more eloquent than words. He was praying for a more than physical strength to control the bitter anger that surged in him.

He had no claim upon her, but the hot surge of emotion in him passed reason. He felt that he had been betrayed by her and then, as the first anger passed, came a bitter feeling that she had betrayed herself into the arms of this man, thinking that she was married to a bestial drunkard. It all came back

93

upon him sickeningly. He had saved the man whom now he wished dead above all other men in the world.

"This is the man, Beatrice," went on Crawford. "This is the man through whom I am going to win out. This is the hammer with which I am going to beat these miners into submission. Donnelly is as helpless as a child before them. I wouldn't be of any use if I were well. Gilson will tame them. He's the man. If only you could have seen him." A smile of almost malicious enjoyment straightened his lips as he spoke.

"Hush!" said Beatrice. "You are worn out now. You are as feeble as a child from the excitement. How can I ever get you well if you do things like this?"

She said this in a tenderly scolding tone whose every syllable stung Newlands like a scorpion lash. He had not forgotten her during these weeks, but his old memory of her was obscured by the evil of his own intentions, for the thing we injure we can never love.

But now, as he watched her at these little domestic duties, he saw her with new eyes. Her hand was busy smoothing out the pillow and tucking the clothes in under Crawford's arms. Once, it seemed to him to linger through an infinitesimal space across the sick man's forehead. He had never seen that hand before, it seemed to him, so white, so slender, the fingers every one so delicately tapering and yet distinct with womanly strength. It seemed to him that hand represented in miniature the whole body of the woman, graceful, tender, beautiful, and strong with a strength of which he had no knowledge before. He turned suddenly and stared out through the door. There heaved the honest mountains, ridge on ridge, proud, self-sufficient, eloquent in silence. When he turned back, he was sure of himself again.

Crawford had apparently not heard Beatrice's injunction

for silence. He was studying Gilson. "I suppose you don't like questions, Gilson," he said.

"I do not," said Newlands quietly.

"Very well, then. There sha'n't be any. You look the part of a miner, all right, but half an eye can see that you're something more. But that is from the point. I don't want to ask you, either, why you volunteered to stand by me today. All I know is that I see in you the one man who can help me in this need I have. Will you do it?"

Beatrice had gone from the room to the kitchen, and now there came a stir of tinware, and over it the soft sound of her voice singing. Newlands sat down in a chair and leaned forward with his elbows on his knees and his fingers strongly interwoven.

"I think I desire to help you," he said slowly.

"Good," said Crawford, "and you can do it! No other man I know is of any use. You know the conditions I work under. I have staked everything here on a theory. If I succeed, I am rich and famous. If I fail, I become the laughingstock of every mining engineer in California. A joke!"

Newlands thought the words over slowly. A joke. A laughingstock. Then failure meant that Crawford would lose Beatrice—meant that he once more. . . . Newlands rose and stood with braced feet. "Go on," he said.

"I need a driver, a man-killer to help me put this thing through. You are the man. They cowered before you today, a man they had never seen before. Gilson, will you stand by me until we win or fail together?"

Newlands began to pace up and down the room, his head drooped forward between the wide shoulders, and his hands clenched behind his back.

"Even if I took the job," he said, "what could I say to the men? I have told them that I would make a compromise with you. What could I tell them?"

"God knows," answered Crawford. "Tell them anything. Promise them anything. I'm desperate. You'll find a way to handle them that I cannot dream of. I don't know such men. I can't influence them. Gilson, you know you can do it. I give you free rein. Anything you say, I will back up. Gilson, will you stand by me?"

Indeed, Newlands felt that he could handle them. He felt an inexhaustible force within him, a force that should move and sway hundreds as easily as one. But to play into the hands of this man was to lose Beatrice beyond all recall. Win together, Crawford had said. Bah! When Crawford won, Newlands had lost all. He resumed the pacing up and down. "Give me a moment to think it over, Crawford," he said. "God knows I have a lot to think about."

Crawford lay silent, and, as Newlands walked, he could feel the steady eyes following him step by step. So at last he came to a pause at the far end of the room with his hands still clenched behind him, and his shoulders bulging forward, and the arms driven straight downward along his back.

It was in this stance that Beatrice saw him as she glanced through the kitchen door, and the sight made her start with terror. Once before she had seen a man stand in that attitude, a man with broad shoulders like these and with large, blunt-fingered hands. Then she remembered and went sick. It had been Newlands when he was telling her of his life. A moment later, as she glanced at this man's heavy boots, the blue jeans, and remembered the bearded face, lean and hard where Newlands's had been soft, her breath came again, and she went to her work, but still tremulous.

All that long moment, while she stared at him, Newlands was thinking and fighting with himself as he had never fought before, for he had never met an opponent be-

Join the Western Book Club and **GET 4 FREE* BOOKS NOW!**
A $19.96 VALUE!

Yes! I want to subscribe to the Western Book Club.

Please send me my **4 FREE* BOOKS**. I have enclosed $2.00 for shipping/handling. Each month I'll receive the four newest Leisure Western selections to preview for 10 days. If I decide to keep them, I will pay the Special Members Only discounted price of just $3.36 each, a total of $13.44, plus $2.00 shipping/handling ($19.50 US in Canada). This is a **SAVINGS OF AT LEAST $6.00** off the bookstore price. There is no minimum number of books I must buy, and I may cancel the program at any time. In any case, the **4 FREE* BOOKS** are mine to keep.

*In Canada, add $5.00 shipping/handling per order for the first shipment. For all future shipments to Canada, the cost of membership is $16.25 US, which includes shipping and handling.
(All payments must be made in US dollars.)

NAME: _____

ADDRESS: _____

CITY: _____ STATE: _____

COUNTRY: _____ ZIP: _____

TELEPHONE: _____

E-MAIL: _____

SIGNATURE: _____

If under 18, Parent or Guardian must sign. Terms, prices, and conditions subject to change. Subscription subject to acceptance. Dorchester Publishing reserves the right to reject any order or cancel any subscription.

fore as strong as his own conscience.

If he refused Crawford, the man was ruined. That was obvious on the face of it. If he accepted and took up the work only half-heartedly, he was still ruined. If he went at it with all his force, Crawford was probably saved, and saved to become rich and make Beatrice happy. Yes, that was the point—Beatrice would be happy with him.

He remembered her face as her hand lingered across Crawford's forehead a moment before. Undoubtedly she loved this man as she could never love him. He remembered the horror with which she had looked out at him when he stood reeling in the aisle beside her berth. He remembered his own face when he had looked at it the next morning in the pool. Could she ever find content with him? Could those white hands ever be cool upon his knotted forehead? He commenced to say over and over again to himself like a child saying a prayer: *It is better for her. It is better for her. It is better for her.* After that he suddenly felt stronger and a glow came through him. This man was strong and clean of heart, while he. . . .

He threw back his head, and Crawford started. He could not tell whether the sound he heard had been a laugh or a groan. Even Beatrice in the kitchen raised her head and half shuddered unawares.

"I'll be your man," said Newlands. "I'll fight for you and be your man until this game is won or lost. They sha'n't ride over me."

Crawford said nothing, but stretched out his hand to Newlands.

"By God, Gilson," he said at last, "you are a man! You'll not lose by this, I swear to you. If the lode is uncovered . . . I'll be able to give you enough shares of stock to make you rich for life . . . and I'll do it."

Newlands's hand had closed over Crawford's, although he did not look him in the eye, but at this their eyes met and Newlands's hand fell away.

"It's all wrong, Crawford," he said. "I won't do this for money. God knows just why I'm doing it. I think it is because you are the underdog. You are making the uphill fight against the big odds, and I like to see short-enders win. It is because I think I see here everything against you with nothing in your favor save a ghost of chance. A ghost of chance! I'll work for that chance, but if you win, I never want to see a cent of the money you make. It's the danger that wins me to you, Crawford, not the money . . . the danger and the ghost of chance!"

Crawford studied him for a moment dubiously and shook his head, but he was obviously too physically weak to debate the matter in his own mind.

"Whatever way you want it, partner," he said. "I only know I'm glad to have you with me. I see the light at last. I don't care what your reasons are for staying, as long as you stay. You'll talk to the men tonight?"

"Yes," Newlands agreed. "I'll talk to them as they've never been talked to since their daddies took them out into the woodshed. I'll talk to them all right. After that, I have to go down to Crackens to send a message . . . that is, if I succeed in quieting the men. Good bye."

Chapter Eleven

THE BITTERNESS OF VICTORY

Newlands did talk to them that night. He waited until they had finished their supper and were sitting about the bunkhouse, smoking their pipes. Then Newlands stood up on the end of one of the tables and called for attention. He got it at once with a sudden turning of heads and puffing of pipes that showed that the men awaited something important.

He had nothing significant to say, but what he could say he would say in a significant way in words of one syllable that everyone could follow. It was a bitter moment for him, standing before that crowd to fight the battle for the man who possessed the woman whom he knew now he loved more than life, and in the little moment, while the stir died out through the room, he was saying over and over to himself, behind clenched teeth, the little formula which he had found earlier in the day: *It is better for her. It is better for her.*

"Boys," he began at last, and his voice sounded strange in his own ears, "when I went up the hill this afternoon to the cabin over there with Crawford, after you fellows had tried to mob him, and come within an ace of doing it, a woman came into the room and brought a tray to him with something to eat." He paused and ground a hand across his forehead as the picture came home to him again. "I suppose all you fellows have seen her about the cabin," he went on, "but I didn't know her. All I knew the moment I laid eyes upon her was that the only thing she is living for is to bring Steve Crawford back to life. She had no eyes for anyone else in that room. She had no smiles for anyone except Steve. And from the way Steve's glance kept following her around the room, it was easy to see that he had formed the habit during the days when she was leading him back from death to life. She meant life to him then. She means happiness and life to him now.

"I suppose all you fellows know what I found out this afternoon. After the wreck at Crackens a few weeks ago, it was this girl who pulled him together and kept him going through the crisis. Well, boys, you know she's not big. She's just a slip of a girl. She hasn't as much strength in her whole body as I have in this one hand."

He flexed and unflexed the large fingers as he spoke, and the men forgot their pipes to listen.

"I'm asking you what it was that made her strong enough to bring Steve Crawford back to life when the doctor gave him up. Why, boys, it was love . . . just pure and simple love. She had nothing but that, and it was enough to save a big, strong man for the world. It made her strong to stay up with him three days and three nights. It made her strong to cook for him and sit up with him and care for him like a baby during all this time. Just plain love, boys.

"Now, while I stood there watching her offer him the food and smoothing out his bedclothes, I couldn't help thinking of the little picture I'd seen down here just a few minutes before. It was a picture of a whole roomful of men . . . all you men who sit here now comfortably smoking your pipes . . . a picture of all of you trying to kill the sick man she had brought back from almost certain death. I did a lot of thinking, boys, when I thought of that picture. There was that frail girl who had saved the strong man. There was the strong man she had saved so weak still that he could hardly raise to his lips the food she brought him. And here are you fellows, a whole roomful of you, who had tried to kill him." He included them all in a tense gesture of unutterable scorn. "Why did you want to kill him, boys? I tell you there must be good in a man for whom a good woman will give herself like a slave.

"He never has wronged you. He never has deceived you. He never made out the contracts you signed with the idea of bulldozing you. You all had eyes to read those contracts. Boys, is it worthwhile to go without your booze and your liberty for a few days and live up to your word and keep from breaking the heart of that man up there in the cabin and the heart of the girl who has saved him so far with love?

"Fellows, I've been in lots of fights, and I've never hit a man while he's down. It's a rotten thing to do. It makes you sick the rest of your life to think of it. I tell you if I was the worst enemy that Steve Crawford ever had, I wouldn't jump on him now. I'd see him through till he was strong and had his muscles back, and then, if I had something against him, I'd go up to him and say . . . 'Crawford, damn your heart, stand up and defend yourself like a man, for here's another man who hates every drop of your blood!' Which is the man's way? This way or the other way? Why, fellows, there isn't one of you who hasn't enough real heart to see the right and the wrong of this thing.

"Think of the little woman up there slaving for the life and happiness of this man, and then of the rest of us, great hulking men able to swing a sledge-hammer all day long. Are we going to work with her or against her? Boys, every one of you who is willing to stick by Steve Crawford and see him make or break on the old Victory, stand up on your hind legs!"

He had built up to his grand climax so suddenly that the miners were on their feet in a moment, swept away by the emotion of the second. But even as they roared their applause, Newlands saw that his game was not yet quite won, nor Beatrice, perhaps, wholly lost to him, and even amidst the cheering the crisis came.

Big Georgeson rose and stalked forward. "Wait a minute, boys," he called, "this here game ain't finished yet! Don't let this guy bulldoze you with a lot of hot air. What has he given us now but a lot of hot air? That's what I'm asking you."

The crowd turned to the new speaker with almost as much interest as they had paid Newlands. The latter saw that he must shut up this speaker at once. If he failed, he was lost as surely as Donnelly was lost before them, and he could never get the power back.

Newlands strode to the orator and smote him heavily upon the shoulder. "Georgeson," he roared, so that every man in the room could hear him, "you're a quitter and a yellow dog!"

Georgeson turned and glowered at Newlands. Tall as the latter was, he was overshadowed by this giant.

"You're a quitter," repeated Newlands steadily, "and a yellow dog!" He pointed his words by striking Georgeson with his open hand across the cheek. The blow sounded through the room like the crack of a whip.

In reply to it Georgeson grunted like a hurt animal and lunged straight at Newlands. It had been Newlands's hope that the miner would know little about the manly art of self-defense, but in this hope he saw he was mistaken, for the very first punch Georgeson sent toward him was a perfect straight left, with his whole body in line behind it. He side-stepped that punch and uppercut with his right as Georgeson lunged past him. The blow made the blond head jerk back.

Then began a fight that more than anything else kept the miners happy during the rest of their stay in the mine.

Georgeson had the strength, the reach, and some science,

but he lacked the tiger-like ferocity of Newlands combined with his coolness and judgment. Where Georgeson rushed and slammed with both hands at every opening, Newlands danced away, waiting always for an opening, with hands poised and always with the curious smile of the fighting man curving his lips. The one man fought with a bull-like straight-forwardness. The other struck when he seemed to be running away, and his punches came straight and short, smashing blows that shook the giant to his feet, doubled him with drives to the body, and sent him staggering with hooks and uppercuts to the head.

In the end Georgeson became wild. A gash over his right eye blinded him with blood, and he began to lose his sense of direction. Then he started large roundabout swings that would have floored a dozen Newlands had they landed. But they never reached a vulnerable spot. Finally Newlands picked his chance and stepped in under a great swing, driving his right hard against the jaw.

Georgeson went down in a heap, and the yelling miners whooped their delight.

But it was Newlands who drove them out of the mess hall and set out by himself to bring the miner back to life with copious drenchings of water. At last the big fellow sat up weakly and stared in a daze at his conqueror. It took a moment for him to recall what had happened, and then he started fiercely to his feet.

The fight was not yet gone from him, and, as Newlands looked at the blazing eyes in front of him, an inspiration came. If he let this fellow go in his present mood, he would stir up new dissension within twenty-four hours.

"Steady, Georgeson," he said calmly, "the luck was against you in that bout, but that's no reason why you should act like a child. It just happened that I had the luck and landed the punch. If things had gone differently, I might just as well have been getting up after a knockout with you standing here."

Georgeson relaxed his hands and stood half reeling and frowning at this grim-eyed man, who looked at him without contempt and without fear, as if they had never fought at all.

It required some time and a great deal of tact, but at last Newlands won out. He told Georgeson that what Crawford needed to keep on running the mine was just such help as he could give. He asked him to form an alliance with him in secret and to use his influence over the men to keep them contented.

The plan worked better than he had dared to dream it might. At first, Georgeson was naturally suspicious, but he could not stand out against the obvious sincerity and frankness of the new boss. Moreover, he still had a wholesome respect for the smashing weight and hardness of Newlands's fists. When he stepped out of the mess hall a few minutes later, he was firmly convinced that Newlands was the greatest man in the mountains and he was ready to demonstrate his conviction on the body of any disposed to argue the matter.

With the new victory listed to his credit and a clear way to success open to him, the strength ran like water from Newlands. The excitement of the affair and his own strong resolve had carried him along so far, but now he knew that all he had done was simply throwing Beatrice into the arms of Crawford. He knew that Donnelly would have carried the story of his success to Crawford by this time, and the best he could do would be to ring up his home and communicate with Benedict to arrange his affairs for a long absence. He reached the little train just as it was about to start for Crackens on a trip for provisions. When they arrived at the town, he lost no time in finding a long-distance telephone.

It was Benedict himself who answered. Benedict the impeccable, the most silent of valets, whose smiles Newlands could have counted upon the fingers of one hand. Benedict the faithful, the strong of heart. As he stood now at the telephone listening, his dark face lit suddenly with one of those rare smiles that Newlands had so seldom seen.

Jimmy Munroe, standing at the entrance to the parlor a few yards away, with his cigarette still burning between his fingers, watched, and listened, and understood.

Chapter Twelve

JIMMY MUNROE MAKES A JOURNEY

As Munroe listened to Benedict at the telephone, the burning cigarette between his fingers sent up a thin streak of blue-white smoke and the little red rim of fire came closer and closer to his flesh, yet he stood without moving, as if he feared that even a change of his expression would be like a warning to Benedict. And this was the moment, this the information for which he had waited patiently day after day.

Since the disappearance of Beatrice and Newlands after the train wreck, Munroe haunted Newlands's town house. A vague fear had grown up in his mind that the big fellow might be trying to double-cross him, but even if this were the case, he knew that sooner or later Newlands would communicate with Benedict. Consequently he followed the lithe Spaniard like a shadow. This was the easier to do because the valet never willingly left the house of his master, and in that house Munroe had long been a privileged character.

Time and again, as he lounged around after the valet, he espied on Benedict's dark face a glance of unutterable malevolence, yet he knew the servant would never dare to refuse the hospitality of the house to one so deep in his master's confidence. He clung to his purpose, almost blindly confident that sooner or later he would get in touch with Newlands through the valet.

On this night when he heard the telephone ring, he rose in the parlor and stole to the entrance to the hall to watch Benedict as he answered the call. In spite of the dimness of the light he could trace the sudden change in Benedict's face as he answered the telephone, a brightening of the eyes and a little vibrant quality crept into his voice. Munroe knew at once that Newlands was on the wire.

"Yes, sir," ran Benedict's end of the conversation. "I hear you very well, sir. Yes, yes. Victory Mine, sir? Yes. Jim Gilson? Very good, sir. Jim Gilson at the Victory Mine. I understand. I shall not tell anyone. Not even he. Yes, very often. Every day. He shall not know of it. You may trust me, sir. Everything is well. I am glad. I am very glad to hear you, sir. Good bye."

The smile still touched Benedict's face as he hung up the receiver and turned away from the telephone, but as he faced around and met the narrowed eyes of Munroe, his expression changed subtly and grimly. His hands clenched at his sides, his eyes widened, he stood at bay like a challenged animal.

"How is Newlands?" asked Munroe.

"I don't know."

"You weren't talking with him?"

"No."

"Don't lie to me, Benedict." Munroe smiled, convinced now that his supposition had been correct. "I saw you as you talked at the phone. Only one voice on God's green earth could light your face like that. It was Newlands, Benedict. Tell me what he had to say."

Benedict bowed quite low, perhaps to hide the expression of his face or perhaps in apology. "It was not Newlands," he muttered. "He had nothing to say."

"It was not Newlands," mocked Munroe, "and Newlands

had nothing to say! For an experienced valet, Benedict, you are a wonderful ass."

Benedict bowed quickly again and started to slip away down the hall murmuring—"I know nothing."—as he passed.

"Don't go yet," said Munroe. "I want to ask you a few more questions." As he spoke, he reached out and caught Benedict by the shoulder. The effect was astonishing. A wildcat awakened by the touch of a human hand never turned more swiftly with lips grinned back over its teeth.

"Swine," whispered Benedict. "Son of a pig. Keep off your hand."

Munroe leaped a good three paces backward and stared breathlessly at the Spaniard as the nightmare expression faded slowly from his face, leaving it only a little pale to tell of the passing of some murderous emotion.

"By God, Benedict," Munroe said with a faint attempt at hilarity, "if you look at me like that again, I'll sue you for breaking the peace. Well, don't talk if you prefer to be silent. But it means nothing now. I'm not a child. I heard it all. Victory Mine. Jim Gilson. That's it. Newlands is at the Victory Mine under the name of Jim Gilson. I'll find him. Benedict, my gentle cut-throat, when your master rings up again, tell him that Jimmy Munroe is coming to call upon him right away."

He was turning away when Benedict spoke with a strange voice.

"Mister Munroe," he began, "I think you will not want to call upon Mister Newlands, wherever he is. Something tells me that Mister Newlands must be in some place where only a few men would enjoy the climate. I think it would be a very bad place for you, Mister Munroe. A very unhealthy place . . . very."

As he spoke, his lips twisted into a smile so mirthless and

sneering that Munroe started. He made a pace toward Benedict, frowning with wonder.

"Look here, Benedict," he muttered, "what the devil is in you, man? Out with it. Have I ever stepped on your corn in the dark? If you're angry be a good dog and bark."

"I know nothing, sir," said Benedict, relapsing at once into his usual manner of expressionless diffidence.

"But a devil of a lot more than anyone gives you credit for, eh, Benedict?"

"I cannot tell, sir, except. . . ."

"Ah, now we have it. Go on."

"Except that I am sure that you would not enjoy yourself where Mister Newlands may now be, sir."

For a moment Munroe stood staring at Benedict and rubbing his chin slowly with one hand. As Benedict spoke, a faint smile had touched his lips and lighted his eyes strangely. It took Munroe far back and across the seas to another country. He shrugged the memory away with a half smile.

"Somehow I believe you, Benedict, old sport," he said, "but I'm built on the lines of a greyhound with a bulldog's heart, Benedict. And when I set my jaws on a bit of easy money, there's no one in the world who can pry them loose, not even you, my dear boy. Yet I hate to leave you behind in this frame of mind. I'd rather walk into a tarantula than meet you in the dark. Good bye, Benedict. I'll be with your master before many hours!"

Munroe was troubled more than he could put into words. He was not a coward. He had met many a danger face to face, but in the presence of this silent malevolence he felt helpless. Therefore he paused when he was halfway down the front steps and looked back to where Benedict was standing with the door slowly closing upon him.

He would have parted with some jest. He even regretted

that he had not tipped the valet with a gold piece. But the sight of Benedict's expression checked him, and, as he heard the door click, he could almost see the lips grin back over the teeth again and hear the whispered cursing.

As he walked down the street, he was trying hard to remember something, some old picture that lay somewhere in the files of his memory—a darkly smiling face and the glint of side-glancing eyes. But he had too many things before him to waste much time on an abstract worry.

The first news he gathered was not particularly encouraging. Through a broker-friend who handled a great many mining stocks, he learned that the Victory was a mine far away in the heart of the Sierras, near the little town of Crackens. He did his best to find out if there was a summer resort of any nature near the mine, but as far as anyone knew, the region had never been popular because of the extreme ruggedness of the mountains. This discovery disheartened Munroe, and for a time he was about to give up his proposed journey. That Newlands should be living at some resort under a different name was quite probable, but that he should actually be in a mine was more than he could understand. It was the ever-present hope of the twenty-five thousand that finally determined Munroe to take this faint chance.

Crackens lay in the hollow of a wedge-like gulch, split through the heart of the mountains. The bottom of the gulch was wide enough to form the single winding street of the village, and the shanties that lined the street straggled up the mountainside at such ludicrous angles that they seemed to be leaning back for support. The only building that appeared at all habitable was a square-frame structure which displayed a battered square sign in front with the inscription: **Al Byron's Hotel**.

On closer approach Munroe discovered that this building comprised no fewer enterprises than a general merchandise and grocery store, a post office and drug store, and a hotel that occupied the second floor, and above all a barroom of really comfortable dimensions. Munroe discovered that this was also the office of the manager, who paused in the midst of his task of spinning out whisky bottles and glasses to a long line of men from the neighboring mines long enough to shove the register toward him.

He turned the stained pages until he came to the last entry, and then signed: **James Gurney, Salt Lake City**. When he asked to be shown the way to his room, the proprietor merely grinned and tossed him the key, pointing toward the stairs that rose from one corner off the barroom.

The room that corresponded with the number of his key was not fitted to improve his mood. The chair, washstand, and bed all bore the marks of age and ill usage. From the ceiling loose ends of wallpaper descended, and the paper on the wall was evilly stained in great parallel streaks as if the rain had found a ready way through the roof. He went to the window to seek some relief in the view.

On either hand the slant mountains leaped at the sky with every jagged rock pointing steeply up, and, as his eye fell back from their sheer ascent to the miserable street below him, it seemed that the dwellings of the men were mere shadows of reality that had taken refuge for the moment in the throat of the gorge and would a moment later be swept away in headlong ruin by some clean wind. Even as he watched that wind arose.

It came shouting from the north and swept over the peaks, with it a marching array of battle-fronted clouds. In a few moments the sky was black, and then the thunder came, long velvet murmurs that drew closer and closer and finally barked and bellowed in his very ear, while the lightnings leaped from cliff to cliff and fell jagged into the gloom of the down-pouring rain.

As Munroe gazed out on this tumult, a great sense of hopeless weakness came on him. That he should be there at all was folly. That he should have come to this wilderness to find a man was absurd.

Finally he fled from his own thoughts downstairs into the barroom again. There were fewer people in the room by this time, for it was late in the afternoon and most of the men had started back toward their mines. Those who were there were unconsciously oppressed to silence by the outroar of the storm. Munroe took advantage of the quiet to ask the bartender if he knew whether or not they were taking on many men at the Victory Mine.

The bartender paused in the midst of a stroke with his cloth across the moist surface of the bar, already worn almost bare of varnish by frequent ineffectual polishings. He fixed Munroe with a keen eye. "Sure they do," he said at last. "Anyway, they're on the hunt for men up at the Victory. Got to sign a funny contract, but you grab down the soft coin up there. After the big money?"

"That's it." Munroe smiled. "The money talks pretty loud to me. Have a drink yourself."

The bartender poured a dash of whisky in the bottom of a glass, waved it in brief acknowledgment to Munroe, and with the same movement downed his drink. "Can you push a pen?" he inquired with more interest.

"Sure," said Munroe.

"Then you might get a pipe job," said the bartender. "Last time Georgeson was down here, he said Crawford . . . that's the nut who runs the joint . . . wanted a sort of clerk."

"Who's Georgeson?" queried Munroe.

"He's one of the bosses," said the other. "Generally gets down here every afternoon after supplies or something."

"I don't know how good I'd be at a pick and shovel," Munroe confessed. "But I guess I could get by with the figure stuff. Can this man Georgeson take me on?"

"Sure he can if he likes you," said the bartender, and he leaned a little more confidentially close. "Let me hand you a tip, bo. If you want to get on the easy side of Georgeson, give him a chance to talk about Gilson. That's another guy at the mine. He's the head boss. Georgeson thinks Gilson is the nephew of God, or maybe His uncle. Gilson's the man who gave him his job, and he's sure proud of it. Here comes Georgeson now."

Munroe turned and saw the doors swing open upon the figure of a tall fellow who came striding in, swinging the water off of his hat, and stamping it out of his heavy boots. He came to the bar and slapped his hand upon it with a force that made it shake.

"Drinks up!" he called in a booming voice. "Liquor up, boys. It's too wet outside to keep dry inside."

Chapter Thirteen

A GHOST FROM THE PAST

There was an immediate mustering to the bar at this welcome summons, and Munroe took care to get the place beside the young Hercules. The bartender took care of the introduction while he was spinning glasses and bottles to the thirsty ones.

"Here's a chap that wants a job," he said to Georgeson. "Can you fix him up?"

Georgeson turned his head and stared down at Munroe. Then he reached up and took the hand that Munroe rested on the bar and turned it palm up, running a rough forefinger across the uncalloused skin.

"Not a hope," he said. "Why, m'son, you'd last about ten shakes in a gang with Jim Gilson drivin' you. The pick would wear clear through to the bone on hands like them."

"I guess neither your friend Gilson nor anyone else would drive me as hard as that," ventured Munroe.

In his attempt to draw out Georgeson he succeeded perfectly. The latter turned his head a moment and stared down at Munroe again as if he could hardly credit his ears. Then he burst into a hearty and not ill-natured laughter.

"There's a lot of 'em talk that way before they see Gilson," he said. "An' there's even some that talk that way after they see him. But once they've got a line on him in action there ain't no talkin' at all. Take it straight from me."

"That sounds pretty violent," Munroe commented. "But I've heard of violent guys before, and they've never scared me a lot. Can you tell me about Gilson?"

"Partner," said the tall miner with an answering grin, "this here day ain't long enough for me to tell you all I know about Jim Gilson. If you was to ask me to describe a balmy day with a tornado hidden away on the edge of the sky, I might get away with it. Or I might be able to tell you all about a snowstorm in the middle of a May day, or a landslide in the middle of the night. But there ain't enough of the old Shakespeare in me to describe this guy Gilson."

"Seems to me you've made a pretty good start," Munroe countered judiciously. "Is he a large man?"

"Not very," Georgeson answered. "He ain't as big as I am, not by quite a lot. I don't reckon he weighs much over two hundred, but it's all condensed meat, partner, like wildcat muscle. He's smooth, that's what he is. And he's got a smooth tongue and pleasant smile and two-thirds of old hell locked up right behind his teeth all the time." He drew a deep breath of reminiscence, and downed his drink at a motion.

"What does Gilson look like?" inquired Munroe, feeling that the information he had gleaned from the overheard telephone conversation must have been correct after all, although why Newlands should be working in a mine was past his wildest conjecture.

"Square-jawed," answered Georgeson, "black-haired, short, thick beard."

"Beard?" said Munroe. "Any mustache?"

"Nope," said Georgeson. "Just a beard. Don't know what else to say about him. It ain't what he looks like, but what he does that makes Jim Gilson. There's a funny, quick way he has about his eyes, though, that I'd be able to pick out of a crowd any time. They get bright and then dark all in a minute."

That was sufficient for Munroe. He had noted the same thing in Newlands a hundred times when the man was excited. He frowned consciously to cover his exultation.

"I'd like mighty well to work near a man like that," he said at last. "What's the chance on this clerking job Bill there was telling me about?"

"I dunno," said Georgeson. "But if you'd really like to work around a bear of a guy like Gilson, I'll take you up. You'll have to see the boss about this job, though. Come up with us on the train. We load her up tonight and run back with her tomorrow morning. Then you can talk to Crawford."

Munroe accepted without too much show of enthusiasm, but he was deeply excited. When he went to bed that night, he lay awake for a long time, for the wind moaned and whistled through the room and his own thoughts kept a fierce accompaniment.

He felt that he was approaching a climax of his life. To be sure Gilson might not be Newlands after all, in spite of the clues of the overheard telephone conversation and the vaguer hints of Georgeson's description. In that case, all his expectation would be for nothing. But the chances were large that this was the man of his quest. If it should prove so, he knew that his task would prove dangerous in the extreme, for, although in the past he had always been able to handle the big fellow, he knew that the day might easily arrive when Newlands would see through him. Yet he would not turn back after going so far.

He was more cheerful when he woke in the morning. The storm clouds had been brushed away by the wind during the night, and the clearness of the day gave him heart. He ate his breakfast hastily, paid his bill, and reached the train on the little siding just before it was ready to pull out for the mine.

While the little engine was groaning and twisting its way up the valley toward the Victory Mine, carrying Munroe toward a strange destiny, and bringing a new twist of fate to the lives of Beatrice and Newlands, Beatrice herself was taking the step that was to involve Crawford finally with the lives of the other three.

She stood at the entrance to the kitchen polishing up the last of the breakfast dishes, and Crawford sat in a roughly improvised invalid chair that some of the mine carpenters had built for him. He was rapidly recovering from his illness and in a few days would be walking around the camp. His face was brightly flushed now, for Donnelly had just left after making an enthusiastic report, and some specimens of rock lay in his fondling hands.

"It is the real quartz?" asked Beatrice.

"No doubt about it," Crawford answered with conviction. "Of course, we've struck the vein here before, and so has everyone else who has started to work the mine. The significant thing is the way the vein peters out and reopens again. According to the look of things now, we are on the verge of the big strike. Just how big no one can tell, but I think it will be big enough to turn this mining district upside down."

"But isn't there enough now to make a satisfactory report to your investment company?" asked Beatrice.

Crawford dropped his chin into the hollow of his hand and frowned. "I wonder," he muttered. "No, not yet. Of course, it looks to me as if we were about to open up the real thing, but it might be only another scare such as we've had before, with nothing coming out of it. I still have nearly twenty days on the lease, and within that time something must develop, or else there is nothing to develop."

"Twenty days," Beatrice sighed, folding her hands together half in anxiety and half in smiling expectation. "Something must show in that time. If only the men can be held together to work until the last moment. Do you think that they can be?"

"I believe they will stay"—Crawford nodded—"for they have found their master at last, and they recognize the fact. Gilson is a god to them, and they work three times as hard for him as they ever would for me. He mixes among them and works with them. Donnelly says that to see him among them you would think that he was one of the lot. But the man's diction is too pure, and his executive power is too fine . . . he is not a simple miner. He has a history behind him, but what it is I can't imagine."

"I have only seen him twice," Beatrice stated, "but I have seen an attraction about him. Once I thought . . . just for a moment . . . that he reminded me of a man I once knew." She caught her breath lightly, as if in pain.

"There is a touch of strange sadness about him," mused Crawford, "a deep melancholy.

"Often, when he reports to me, he will not look me in the eye. It is as if he found something he hated in both me and in his work. And other times he has stared at me so fixedly and with such an unusual brightness of eye that the shivers have gone up and down my back. By Jove, what a man! But a leader, a born leader, if ever I saw one."

"Yes, yes!" cried Beatrice. "I can understand why the men will follow him. There is something in the very set and bulge of his shoulders, in the masterful uplift of his chin, in the big, square-tipped fingers that is instinct without self-possession. He will surely hold the men together. He'll win the fight for you."

She had finished her work, and now she came and stood beside his chair, the palm of her hand resting on the woodwork, and the tips of her fingers as light as a caress upon his shoulder.

"How very happy it all makes me," she murmured. "I don't see how we could be happier, do you?" She leaned down somewhat as she said this and saw that Crawford's face had darkened swiftly. She could even feel him shrink under her touch. With a little pang of understanding she stepped away from him. "I'm sorry I said that," she said softly, "so very sorry."

"Don't be sorry," he said rapidly, after a moment of pause. "Don't be sorry, Beatrice, but give me permission to open the old subject just this one time more. Then, if you will, we shall forget it forever."

As he turned his head, he saw that she stood somewhat away from him with her head thrown back and strained as if against an invisible power. As if in self-protection her hand had fallen against her breast.

"I had rather that you did not speak of it," she said at last. "I had so much rather. We were happy just now, but when you spoke of the other thing, it can only make us both sorrowful."

"I will not say a word about it if you wish me to be silent," Crawford said, but, as he spoke, his hand went out to her in unconscious entreaty.

She weakened with compassion before the gesture. "If you really wish to talk it all over again," she said, "I will not forbid you." She went to him and laid her hand impulsively on his shoulder. "But it is hardly fair to you," she said, "for you can never win out against a hopeless obstacle. You never can!"

Crawford's hand went up and imprisoned the slender fingers at his shoulder.

"There isn't any obstacle in the world that is impossible," he declared, "and I know that nothing shall keep you from me the moment I have won your love. At the least you can tell me that, Beatrice. You can tell me whether or not you have come to care for me. Don't lie to me because you think I am physically weak now. I tell you I am always strong to hear the truth! Say it out frankly and I'll get well all the quicker. If you do not care for me at all, if you feel that you can never come to care for me as I want you to, tell me, and I'll get over the hurt of it in my own way."

She trembled before the eager entreaty of his eyes.

"It is so hard for me to talk with you about it," she said. "So hard, that you can never imagine. If I say that I do not love you, it is not the whole truth. If I say that I can never come to love you, it is very, very far from the truth. And the truth is the best, isn't it, Steven?"

"Beatrice," he whispered. "Then you do care for me a little . . . you feel that you could come to care for me more?"

"Oh!" she cried, suddenly breaking away from his hand, and throwing up one arm across her eyes as if to shut out her own thoughts. "How can I talk to you about it? I tell you that I have no right. If you wish to hear the whole thing, then let me go into my past and show you how impossible it all is. You would never let me tell about the past before. Will you let me now?"

The assent moved Crawford's lips, but before the words came, he shook his head vigorously. "It is not right to tell me what has happened in your past," he declared. "I don't care what has happened, and I can imagine things far more horrible than any that have happened to you. All I know and care is that I am mad for you, hungry for you and for your love as you are this moment here before me. I know what you are. Why should I care for what you have been? Oh, my dear, don't you see that the past is nothing? That our lives look forward and upward like that range of mountains, Beatrice?"

She dropped her arms straight down by her sides and clenched the hands. "You must hear me!" she pleaded.

"Not a word," he said firmly. "It is childish of you to insist upon it. You know that I am right."

She moved her hand helplessly. "It is so different from anything that you dream!" she cried.

"Is it anything that cannot be undone?"

She had thought vaguely before of taking steps toward a divorce, but had always shrunk from the thought. Now it seemed a happier possibility. She turned to Crawford with a somewhat brighter face.

"I . . . I think it might be undone," she said. "I cannot tell about such things."

"No more about it," commanded Crawford. "That is all I want to know. The point now left between us is whether or not you think that you could ever come to care enough for me to be my wife. Beatrice, tell me that as frankly and as bravely as you can."

"There are a thousand doubts like mists across my mind," she said. "How can I tell? How can I read the future? I know that you have been very dear to me. I know that when you were first hurt and lay in the long delirium for days and days I would gladly have given my life to bring yours back."

He caught her hand and pressed it against his eyes, and she looked down on him with infinite tenderness and let her other hand caress his hair.

"Yes, yes," she went on with slowly wandering eyes that told that her heart was deeply moved. "You were very dear to me, then. Oh, I have yearned over you in your sleep like a mother over a child and prayed for your strength to come back . . . and the clearness to your mind. And when the delirium passed, it seemed as if God had answered my prayers and that He had permitted me to succeed in the greatest work of my life." She bent back his head gently and looked in his eyes. "It is such a wonderful thing," she said, "for a simple girl such as I to keep the life in the body of a great, strong man such as you, Steven . . . such a very wonderful thing." She sighed, and, as her eyes wandered slowly away again, a dim smile touched her mouth and changed it. And then again her breath caught. "But it is not love," she said. "Oh, it is not love!"

Strangely enough she half shuddered as she spoke, and Crawford wondered. He could not dream that she was thinking of Newlands, of the intense black eyes, or the strained hands that had touched her very soul through her body. Remembering it now, she knew that was love, perhaps the physical part of love only, but something so intense and vital that it made her tremble.

"Not love?" said Crawford. "Perhaps not love. I do not ask that you love me all at once. All great things come slowly, Beatrice. When I saw you at first, I did not love you, but as my eyes followed you day by day, I came to know that I could never be truly happy without you. How I need you, Beatrice, how utterly I need you! Oh, my dear, I love you so much that in time you will be sure to love me a little. The large grows out of the small." He paused a little, and he could see that she was troubled.

"There is another thing which we surely must plan against," he continued rapidly, "and that is the fact that you are living here as my wife. The men suspect nothing. It would be very bad if we let fall some clue that would start their imaginations. It would be ruinous, perhaps, to your future in case we do not marry. But we must marry, dear. Don't you see how everything points to it? Fate is with me now. And I need you so!"

"Do you think that I could really help you?" she asked.

"Do you think that I could really join you in your problems?" As she spoke, she was seeing him as on the first day in the train when he bent over the blueprints, his forehead knotted in study.

"Yes, yes!" he cried. "All things turn my way now. It is the tide in my affairs! First when I am hurt almost to death in a wreck, it is a woman who saves me and brings me back to life and work. Then when I am out to lose my men at the mine and lose all my hope of fortune and success with them, there comes a black-browed hero from nowhere and stands between me and them. Yes, becomes my right-hand man, molds those hordes of big-handed laborers to his will, rules them like a Napoléon, and in the end shall win my battle for me.

"Beatrice, he will tear the heart out of that mountain yonder and give it to me, and I in turn will place it at your feet. I tell you there is such a thing as fate, for only fate could have sent you to me . . . you and Gilson in the crisis of my life."

She had pushed herself somewhat back from him with her protesting hands, but he pressed her closer and closer, and her arms trembled.

"Fate cannot go wrong," Crawford insisted. "I would not have been given this promise of happiness if the reality did not lie close behind. Beatrice, say that you can learn to care for me, that in time you will marry me."

She dropped to her knees beside his chair. "God help me to do and say the right thing," she whispered, so softly that Crawford could scarcely hear her, "but I do care for you now, and in time I hope that I may be able to learn to love you. Does that content you?"

His first impulse was to gather her in his arms, but, noting her shrinking, he merely kissed her forehead. She laughed tremulously at his eagerness, and afterward she brushed her lips lightly against his.

But the laughter was not altogether happy. She was strangely excited now that she had taken the final step, and the excitement brought into her mind a disturbing picture. Above all, at the very moment when she kissed him came the controlling image of Newlands, the command of those deep eyes, the tensed and plundering lips. It fell across her life as a shadow falls upon a sunlit pool.

Perhaps it was because she wished to drive away these thoughts that she commenced to sing. It was a gay, trilling song, and the sound ran afar through the mountain air, sometimes lost in a stir of the wind, and sometimes troubled with echoes.

It fell waveringly upon the ear of Jimmy Munroe on his way from the train to the cabin that Georgeson had pointed out to him. He stopped short and listened with a deep wonder that grew from moment to moment.

Chapter Fourteen

A MESSAGE IN THE CARDS

He set the voice down as belonging to Mrs. Crawford, for on the way up from Crackens, Georgeson had named her as the only woman at the mine and dwelt upon her for some time with his clumsy adjectives.

But Munroe himself could not have told why he stopped to listen until the song had died away, a thin, sweet singing through the solemnity of the mountains. Perhaps it was because he was not quite sure as to the identity of the voice. Perhaps it was because through that moment a dim debate went on in his heart and the eternal yes and no of conscience troubled him. Then, once the sound ceased, he knew where he had heard the voice before. It had come faintly down from the room of Beatrice at *Madame* Fenwick's, after the wedding. The same voice, the same song, but in these surroundings how different it was.

It made his mind swim at first. If it was indeed Beatrice, then how could she be living here as the wife of Crawford? And if she lived here, how could Newlands be at the same mine under a different name? The whole thing was a mighty puzzle to him. As he took up his way toward the cabin, he nerved himself to be strictly on his guard.

Yet when he came opposite the open door of the cabin and, looking through, saw Beatrice for a moment at the entrance to the little kitchen, his heart stopped. It was unquestionably she.

He had to pause a moment before he could go on. To be sure he had been very efficiently disguised when he had acted as minister on the day of the fraudulent wedding, yet there was always a gambling chance that she should recognize him by his voice or some trick of expression. But he had gone too far to turn back now at the last moment. He stepped up and knocked boldly at the door.

"Come in!" called a man's voice, and at the same moment he saw Beatrice reappear for a moment and look at him curiously from the kitchen entrance.

With a great effort he drew his eyes away from her and stepped into the open door with his cap in his hand. There he found Crawford seated in the invalid chair, facing him.

"I suppose," Munroe began, "that you are Mister Crawford?"

"I am," said Crawford.

"My name is James Gurney," Munroe said smoothly. "I came up on the train with Georgeson from Crackens. I met him down there yesterday, and he said that you were looking for a good accountant. He said he'd let me come up here on the train, but that, if you didn't take me on, I'd have to walk back to Crackens because no men were allowed to idle around the mine."

"That's right," said Crawford. "I'm rather surprised that Georgeson allowed you to come up on the train. But I do want an accountant."

"I'm taking the chance," said Munroe. "If I don't get the job, I'll walk back." He extended his slender hands palms up. "You see I'm not very well fitted for rough work, but I'm pretty fast and accurate with figures."

"I'll have to try you out," Crawford stated. "I want a sort

of housekeeper and bookkeeper, but he has to be pretty fast and straight with figures. Otherwise, I'm afraid you'll have to foot it back to Crackens. Will you give me that black-covered account book on the shelf there, Beatrice?"

She brought him the book without a word, and Munroe rejoiced that her eyes, as they passed him, did not linger, and no sign of recognition lit her face.

"Here you are," said Crawford, opening the book. "Here's a column of figures. Just stand here beside me and run up a few columns."

Years before, while he was working the racetracks as a bookie, Munroe had acquired a remarkable facility in rapid figuring, and it now stood him well in stead. He took his place beside Crawford, took the pencil from the latter's hand, and moved it swiftly up the long columns.

"Nine thousand seven hundred and sixty-one," he said, and passed his pencil to the next group. "Fourteen thousand seven hundred and eighty-eight."

"Wait a minute," Crawford interrupted. "Do you mean to say that you are actually adding? Or are you just guessing?"

"You can easily check the columns." Munroe smiled. "Here's my last four-bits to say that I've added them right." He drew the coin from his pocket and regarded it with a sigh.

Crawford was both touched and surprised. He ran his eyes over the man's rather dilapidated apparel. "I won't check them," he said, "but that's the fastest work I've seen. With such a head for figures, you don't belong in these parts."

"I'm off on my luck," Munroe said solemnly. "I'd take any sort of a job rather than hoof it back to Crackens now."

Crawford considered him severely, but Munroe bore the examination without flinching.

"I guess you'll do," said Crawford. "But we'll have to come to an understanding before you get the job. You'll have to work up here in the day, and you can sleep here at night. I'm about well now, but I have to have someone around all the time in case of need. In other words, you'll have to stick at the cabin all the time. I don't know you, and I can't have men I don't know loitering around the mine or the miners. The men down there are under the eye of Gilson and they're safe enough. But you'll be sleeping here, away from Gilson's eye, and, if I let you go down to the mine, you could easily get away with a lot of important information. Not that I suspect you of spying, but I want you to know where you stand here."

"It's all one with me," said Munroe. "I'd just as soon work in a cave for three squares a day and enough money to get me back to Frisco after a while."

"Good," Crawford said. "Then I'll take you at fifty per and keep. That satisfactory? All right. You can rig up that table over there to work on."

Within half an hour Munroe had arranged his working place and was ensconced behind a pile of books and papers hard at work with his accounting. He spent that afternoon in silence and hard work, and more that evening after Beatrice had left for her own cabin, that stood a little way higher up the hill. When Donnelly and Georgeson brought up their reports from the mine, Crawford asked him to step into the kitchen until the reports had been heard. In the kitchen he glued his ear against a crack and listened, but Crawford talked with his chiefs in such subdued tones that he could only catch meaningless words here and there.

The next day passed in the same manner, and Munroe began to worry. Carefully as he watched for clues that would lead him on the right track toward Newlands, he found nothing. He could not ask outright permission to see Gilson, for this would have made Crawford suspicious. He began to suspect that his only hope was to obtain an interview with

Gilson through a demand upon Beatrice. Yet he hesitated to make this demand.

For all he knew Beatrice had long ago discovered that the wedding was illegal, and, if he mentioned her past, he might implicate himself. To question her was impossible in so delicate a situation. Neither could he gain anything from his observations of the conversations between Beatrice and Crawford.

It was not until the third day that his opening came to probe Beatrice as to what she knew. Another man would not have considered it an opening at all, for Crawford was in the room, but Munroe determined on a plan of indirect querying even in the presence of a third party.

It was the middle of the afternoon when, at the suggestion of Beatrice, the men stopped their work, Crawford pushing aside his blueprints and Munroe his account-books, to drink a cup of coffee. Crawford, who had evidently been attracted by the silent steadiness with which Munroe clung to his task, opened a more friendly conversation, and it was in the midst of this that Munroe, his eye falling upon a pack of cards on the shelf above, received his inspiration. A remark of Crawford's about chance paved the way for him, and a moment later they were discussing fortune-telling.

"I have seen too many prophecies of fortune-tellers come true not to believe in it a little," said Munroe, who had been upholding the second sight against the smiling incredulity of the other two. "To be frank, I've even tried my own hand at it. I don't pretend to have the real gift, but sometimes I've hit it off pretty well."

"Well, then,"—Crawford laughed—"tell me the fate of the Victory Mine."

"That's the trouble," Munroe said with a smile. "I can't talk about the future, but sometimes I can figure out the past pretty well. That's generally considered even harder, isn't it?"

"What fun!" Beatrice exclaimed eagerly. "Will you tell me about my past?"

"Well," murmured Munroe with pretended reluctance, "I can't always hit the truth, and, even when I do, it is all sort of vague and veiled . . . but I'll try if you wish." He took down the pack of cards from the shelf.

"If you have no objection to my wasting some time at this, Mister Crawford," he said apologetically to Crawford.

"Go ahead," said Crawford. "You've already done more work than most men would do in ten days."

Munroe took the cards from the case and shuffled them with the easy skill of the old familiarity. The very touch of the pasteboard gave him a new feeling of power, and he began hastily searching his mind for some recollections of the occult art.

"You see," he began, "I take out all the cards under the seven spots . . . so. Then I shuffle them all again. Now you shuffle them, Missus Crawford, and, as you do, please fix your mind on your past and try to recall all the important events vividly. It's fair to ask that, isn't it?"

"Of course," she answered, interested in spite of herself. As she shuffled the cards, she let her mind wander back over the eventful past until she half closed her eyes with a faint shiver and passed the pack back to Munroe. "All right, Mister Gurney. We are ready for the test."

"I deal them in a semicircle with the center toward me," he went on, frowning intently as he suited the act to the word. "The queen of hearts will be the significator, or, that is to say, the card that has the more direct relation to you. But all the cards in the circle mean something to your past, and each semicircle that I deal out represents a particular moment in your life. Do you understand?"

"Yes, yes," she said, nodding. "I am almost beginning to believe it."

He bent over the cards for a long moment of study. "The first deal is always the hardest," he muttered, and relapsed into a study again. "From the way these cards run from the right to the left," he went on after the pause, "I haven't been able to go back into the past." As he spoke, he turned a little in his chair. "Do you mind if I raise that window and let a bit more air in, Missus Crawford?"

"As you wish," she said.

He rose and walked toward the window. "In fact," he said, as he walked across the room, "the cards read back, apparently only a short time. By the way, Mister Crawford, how long have you been married?" He raised the window noisily as he said this, but it seemed to him that he heard a sudden starting of a chair as if she had half risen. He lingered a moment as if to look out of the window, but, when he turned, he saw the flush still on her face. Munroe knew that whatever else had happened she had certainly not discovered the fake marriage, or at least, having done so, she had not yet married Crawford.

"Just a short time," answered Crawford, and found it necessary to cough immediately.

"Anyway, I'll tell you what the cards say," Munroe began again. "The queen of hearts is way down here at one side of the semicircle, you see? That shows that your happiness was at a pretty low ebb. Yet strangely enough there are two sevens close to you. This indicates plainly enough that you received a legacy at the same time that you were unhappy."

"By Jove!" Crawford laughed. "Think of being unhappy after receiving a legacy. I guess he has missed it that time, eh, Beatrice?"

"Don't stop," she said, leaning far forward across the table. "This is really wonderful. It was just as you say . . . there was a death."

"Really?" said Munroe. "I'm sorry if I've brought up unpleasant memories. But I can't pretend to be one of those optimistic fortune-tellers who talk to you at fairs." He commenced to shuffle the cards again, and then dealt them out in another semicircle.

"Ah," he said, "see where the queen is now! Before she was low down as if your happiness was oppressed by circumstances, but now she is almost halfway up the side of the circle. You are cheering up."

"Perhaps the legacy has helped." Crawford smiled.

"No," pondered Munroe. "I think she has forgotten about the legacy. Something else has happened. Two tens always mean a change, as far as I can make out, and here they are in the corner as big as life. Ah, I see what the change is now. Look, the nine of clubs right at the side of the queen of hearts, the significator. That's a long journey, a journey over the sea. Red and black. I'd wager that the hull or the smokestack of the ship was red and black."

"They were! They were!" cried Beatrice, and she stared at him now with a real awe. "What a remarkable power you have!"

"By Jove," muttered Crawford, "this begins to look almost spooky."

"It is strange how realistically the thing works out sometimes," Munroe stated. "I almost believe it myself, now and then. Of course, it's just chance. The next deal will probably tell nothing."

Again he arranged the cards in the semicircle. "Aha!" he exclaimed. "Happiness at last! Look, the queen is in the very highest point of the arch. Why was that happiness?" He leaned closer over the cards. "A passing love affair . . . see, there's the eight of hearts halfway up the circle. Undoubtedly there was a passing love affair. Begins to look like a history of the heart, Missus Crawford."

As he looked up and smiled at her, he rejoiced to see that she had joined her fingers nervously together and was staring at him half in wonder and half in fear.

"And see over there," he went on, "there's the knave of clubs. Yes, right beside the queen of hearts. That's the man who brought in the happiness. Hmm. Strange enough. . . ." He stopped with affected concern and flashed a glance of hesitation toward Crawford.

"Go on," Crawford urged. "I sha'n't be jealous. Let's hear it out, eh, Beatrice?"

"Of course," she said somewhat faintly. "They are only silly cards."

"Certainly," Munroe agreed, sighing with apparent relief. "Well, this man does not appear to be you, Mister Crawford. Not in the least. Look at that run of cards . . . seven, eight, nine, ten . . . one after another. He was a man of great physical energy, I think . . . a big, powerful man and dark. See, the knave is in a group of dark cards except for the queen of hearts. That's obvious." He picked up the cards and began to shuffle again. "Looks almost like a connected narrative, doesn't it, Mister Crawford?" he asked pleasantly, carefully avoiding the eye of Beatrice.

"Regular illustrated storybook," Crawford commented.

Munroe arranged another semicircle. "This is bad," he said, scowling at the cards. "Three jacks together. That should mean trouble ahead, and yet one of the jacks is the jack of clubs, our dark gentleman who met the lady in the last chapter. Also note that she is still very happy and at the top of the circle. Hmm. I can't make this out. And here's the eight of hearts still higher up than it was last time. The love affair continues and even grows stronger. But right next to the knave of clubs is the seven of spades, which always stands for obstinacy. I guess you were giving the gentleman a bad time. Could you be accused of flirting, Missus Crawford?"

"Of course not." Beatrice laughed, but it seemed to Munroe that there was an hysterical note in her laughter.

He arranged the cards in a new semicircle, and then started a little in his chair. "Well, well," he said, "this begins to get really exciting. Here's that queen still at the top of the arch. She has a long spell of happiness and success, but all around her are the three knaves. Evidently they have made her happy, and they are also preparing trouble for her in the future. You are trying to make up your mind about something. What is it? Yes, yes, I see it now. Look! A proposal!"

"A what?" queried Crawford, and his voice drowned the sound of a suddenly indrawn breath from Beatrice.

"Not a doubt of it," went on Munroe. "Look at the ace of diamonds here with the eight of the same suit beside it. There is a proposal and a good deal of hesitancy, but it looks to me as if the proposal is being accepted. I beg your pardon, Missus Crawford, but, of course, I have to say what the cards tell me."

As he spoke, he looked up and saw that she was quite pale, but making an apparent effort to control herself. He was sorry that he had piled up his effects so rapidly, but as he went on, he became surer and surer that she still believed herself bound to Newlands. Otherwise, her emotion would not have been so real.

Luckily Crawford was growing too much absorbed in the cards to look at Beatrice. Munroe ran out the cards again.

"Behold!" he cried, tossing out the hand in mock triumph. "I was right! There are two tens side by side as big as life. If that doesn't mean a marriage, I'll tear up my cards and never touch them again. A marriage!"

"By Jove," breathed Crawford. "What do you know about that, Beatrice?" He turned toward her, half smiling and half serious, but she had partially shielded her face by leaning her cheek against the palm of her hand.

"At least," she murmured, "it makes a good story."

"Doesn't it?" agreed Munroe heartily, certain now that his surmise was correct, and that she still thought the marriage a real one. "And here for the fourth time the queen of hearts is happily enthroned on the top of the arch, with the eight of hearts on one side, and the knave of clubs on the other. The dark gentleman must have been a wonderful wooer, because he seems to have won out in spite of the fact that it was only a passing fancy."

"I am sorry," sighed Beatrice, "but I must get to work on the supper." She started to rise.

"No, no," Munroe pleaded. "That will break up the story. I really can't find anything to say unless my subject is sitting close to the cards."

"Please stay," Crawford echoed. "I haven't had so much fun in a month. I have something to tease you about now, Beatrice."

She smiled wanly, and reluctantly sat down again.

Munroe ran out the cards hastily. He was determined to clinch his preconceptions before stopping the game. "What's here?" he called, starting again as he stared at the cards. "Oh, this is too bad, too bad. Three knaves again. Yes, and they are right at the top. The trouble winning out. It has come. See, the poor queen of hearts is nearly at the bottom of the circle on the right-hand side. You count from the right to the left, you know, which shows that her trouble is the most important thing. Yes, those were surely unhappy days. And here's the ten of spades near the queen. That surely means an unhappy journey. Looks like an unpleasant honeymoon trip, eh?" He dared not look up to Beatrice now, and continued with bent head, staring at the cards, but he could hear her rapid breathing.

"Gurney," Crawford interrupted, laughing shortly, "you should take up writing. You have enough imagination to succeed at it."

"Not a bit," Munroe assured him seriously, and now out of the corner of his eye he was aware that the hand against Beatrice's cheek was trembling slightly. "I can't say a thing except what the cards tell me." For it had occurred to him as he worked the game that, if he could plant suspicion between Beatrice and Crawford, he would be making his own position stronger later on. He shuffled the cards and dealt again. "I guess I had better stop here," he said as he examined the cards.

"No, no," insisted Crawford, "things are just beginning to get complicated, eh, Beatrice?"

"By all means," she said in a weak voice, and then cleared her throat to cover her nervousness.

"Well, then," went on Munroe, shaking his head, "this looks pretty bad. Very bad. Here's a poor queen of hearts at the very bottom of the circle. She is beaten and broken by circumstance. And look. Four aces in a row! A great shock. Calamity, trouble, confusion, all at once. The poor queen is heartbroken. See, the seven beside the last ace. She even thinks of death. And here is the knave of clubs at the top of the circle still. Evidently the trouble has not affected him. He almost seems to gloat in his happiness, doesn't he? Strange that he should be happy when she is troubled."

"It's a perfect riddle," Crawford stated with interest.

"But here," went on Munroe, "at the very moment when

she is most downcast, comes the great shock . . . what is it? I cannot tell that. I only see the horror and the confusion. Yes, death is very near the queen and the knave, too, and at this very moment there is another man entering . . . look . . . the king of hearts, with the ten of spades and the nine of spades beside him . . . see . . . he is in trouble, too, for he is far down the circle, but he is near the queen. Has he met her? What has happened?"

"My God!" broke in the voice of Beatrice, hoarse and strained with pent emotion.

Both men started up from the table, and Munroe could see that Crawford was almost as pale as Beatrice. She sat with both hands pressed hard against her eyes as if she strove to shut out a memory. In his heart Munroe knew that he had succeeded.

"Beatrice," Crawford said, reaching out from the invalid chair and resting one hand upon her shoulder, "it is all a game of cards. You are not taking this seriously?"

"No, no," Munroe insisted. "It's all a game . . . a jest!"

She drew a long, sharp breath that made a faint hissing through the room, and rose slowly from her chair. Her face was white, and the eyes staring like one who has just looked upon a tragedy.

"I have too much imagination," she faltered. "And . . . and I guess I'm not very well today."

"Let me get you some water," Munroe offered. "Please sit down again." He went hastily into the kitchen.

"No, no," she protested. "I am really all right . . . just a little excited with . . . with your story."

As she came into the kitchen, he met her with concern in his eyes, and held toward her a glass of water. She did not seem to see it.

"Did the cards tell you all that?" she demanded.

Chapter Fifteen

REOPENING A SEALED BOOK

He watched her a moment, wondering how far he could go. "At least," he said, "they told me a great deal more, which I would prefer to tell you when we are alone."

She shrank back a little, and if possible her face blanched still whiter.

"If it can be arranged . . . and you care to hear," he went on softly.

"It must be arranged," she whispered desperately, her eyes turning back toward the open door as if she feared that even these light whispers would be overheard. "They will wheel him down to the mine tomorrow morning. Wait till then."

His face was utterly composed when he stepped back into the next room. Crawford sat leaning somewhat forward in his chair, and, when he raised his face, Munroe saw that it was stricken with pain.

"She seems to be all right now, Mister Crawford," he said pleasantly. "I am very sorry that my little tale should have upset her. Women have such imaginations, you know."

Presently the clattering pans in the kitchen told him that the household had fallen into its accustomed regime.

But with a change, thought Munroe. *Ah, yes, with a change.* And he smiled behind his hand.

He noticed it with his careful eyes the rest of that day and during the supper. There was nothing that a casual observer would have noticed, but little things were beginning to speak volumes to him. When Beatrice moved about the room in the evening after the long silence of the supper, he watched Crawford's hurt stare follow her, to be averted with guilty suddenness the moment her head turned. A dozen times he could trace the grief or pity stirring in Beatrice's face. Decidedly his work had commenced.

He continued his work in the evening by the lantern light in the hope that Crawford would ask some question after Beatrice had left, but although the engineer turned wistful eyes upon him several times, he had too much power of repression to ask the questions that Munroe knew were on his tongue.

The next morning he waited with a growing sense of both expectancy and power for the moment when Crawford should be wheeled off toward the mine. When Georgeson and red-whiskered Donnelly came for him, and Munroe was left alone with Beatrice, he allowed her to open the conversation. He even felt a vague and unpleasurable curiosity as to how she would go about the difficult task. But he had not counted on her natural directness.

She came to his table and stood with the tips of her fingers leaning against the edge, while she looked bravely into his face. "Yesterday," she began in an even voice, "it seemed incredible that the cards should have told you so many interesting things more or less connected with me. It seems even more incredible after I have had the night to think it over. I have come to ask you to be *absolutely* frank with me, Mister Gurney."

He tilted back in his chair and drummed his pencil meditatively against his chin, while he looked up at her.

"Franker than the cards?" he asked.

She studied him a moment rather grimly, and then turned suddenly away and walked across the room to a chair. It was as if she sought temporary safety in the little distance. Now as she faced him again, her hand resting hard on the back of the chair, Munroe felt as if his power were closing around her like a hand from which there was no escape. Yet his face showed no emotion.

"At least," she was saying, "I wish you would tell me just why you have come up here. I am sure it was not for the work."

He had decided to be quite frank with her, for he did not know when someone from the mine would interrupt them, and this might be his last statement. He saw plainly that he must talk with Newlands before he could act intelligently, and, after all, Gilson might not be Newlands.

"My purpose," he said, "is the plainest and simplest in the world. I have come here to see one of the men employed in the mine . . . Jim Gilson."

It was a crucial moment, and he watched her narrowly. But she showed no sign of starting or recognition, only a deeper wonder.

"But Mister Crawford does not allow people to talk with the miners," she protested. "How can you see Mister Gilson?"

He shrugged his shoulders. "I thought that possibly you could arrange that for me."

Sudden intelligence came to her. She started forward toward the table. "I see it very clearly now," she said tensely. "You wish to get information concerning the mine from Mister Gilson. You have known him before. But I tell you he would never give you that information. He is pledged to Mister Crawford."

Munroe leaned forward and spoke frankly, glad that he could speak the clear truth.

"Missus Crawford," he said, "will you believe me when I say that I have not the least concern in the world about the Victory Mine? I will give you my word of honor that I shall not ask Gilson a word about it. Does that make it easier for you to send for him?"

She had twisted her hands together now, and she watched him wistfully. "I wish . . . I wish . . . ," she began, and then broke off with a little gesture of helplessness. "Don't you see that I can't do that? I do not know you. How can I trust even your word? Oh, it endangers so much . . . secrecy is so necessary here. And you might have some hold over Gilson. How can I tell? He is such a strange fellow. No one knows what his past has been."

"Secrecy?" queried Munroe gently, seizing upon that part of her speech. "Is it so vital here?"

"Yes, yes!" she said impatiently. "Don't you see how the miners are guarded almost like criminals?"

"Yes," Munroe responded. "I believe you are right. Secrecy is vital here. Consider last night, when the cards had said so much."

She caught a little breath, and the fright widened her eyes.

"Even the little that the cards hinted seemed to make such a great difference to Mister Crawford, now, didn't it?" he went on easily.

She seemed as if she were about to speak, but she only made a little imploring gesture. He lowered his eyes as if he had not seen it.

"And it occurs to me now that it might be positively embarrassing," he went on, "if Mister Crawford should desire me to take down that pack of cards again."

"You would not . . . ," she began impulsively.

"It is not I," he protested. "But how can I help it if the cards talk? Suppose, for instance, that the cards went on and told more details. Really, I saw so many pictures in those cards that it took my breath away. For instance, I think Mister Crawford would be greatly interested in a further description of the jack of clubs. He was such a big, fine fellow as I saw him. Short-cropped, black mustache, keen eyes, big, square-tipped fingers. You would never believe how clearly I have seen him."

It seemed to him that she was waiting for this speech to sink into her inner mind before she could talk.

"Think how extremely this would interest Mister Crawford."

She watched him, fascinated and dumb.

"Surely," he said, "after I have volunteered so many additions to our little story you will be willing to send for Gilson?"

She stamped her foot, tortured into a sudden anger. "I shall not!" she cried. "I shall not do it! It would be betraying Steven. What a coward you are to ask me to do it. You have no power over me . . . no right to ask this of me."

He saw that she was speaking with a courage that was more hysterical than real, and he decided to make his masterstroke while she was still at the highest pitch of excitement. He rose and bowed to her. "Then I am quite sure I have nothing more to say . . . to you . . . Missus Newlands," he said in an even voice.

Her head fell back as if he had struck her in the face with his clenched hand. She dropped into the chair and lay motionless, her head turned a little to one side, and her arms hanging straight down at her sides. Munroe rose in some concern. She seemed to have broken like a whip handle under too long a lash. Before he could reach her a great, familiar voice boomed a little beyond the door.

"Hallo!" called Georgeson.

Beatrice was shocked erect in her chair at that sound. In his heart Munroe admired her courage with which she met the crisis. She rose slowly from the chair as Georgeson's great frame blocked the doorway.

" 'Mornin', Missus Crawford!" he boomed. "Mister Crawford's down to the mine. He wants to know if you'd care to come down an' take a look through the place this mornin', what?"

She was gripping the back of the chair with white fingers, but even at that moment of stress the face she turned to Georgeson was smiling faintly.

"Tell Mister Crawford that I am too busy this morning," she said in a calm voice. "Some other time I will go."

"Very well, ma'am," said Georgeson, and turned away to go down the hill.

"Remember Gilson, please," Munroe whispered.

She met his eye with a white defiance, but, seeing the set purpose of his face, she threw out one arm in surrender. "Georgeson!" she called.

The big fellow returned and leaned in the doorway.

"Georgeson, will you ask Mister Gilson to step up here? I wish to speak to him just for a moment . . . if he is not too busy."

"Certainly, ma'am," said Georgeson. "Anything else?"

"Nothing, Georgeson . . . and . . . thank you."

He had hardly disappeared again from the door, when the hand on the back of the chair relaxed suddenly and she sank into the seat again, but this time with her head fallen forward in the despair of absolute surrender. Munroe sat with his chin in his hand and watched her.

She rose. "I must not be here when he comes," she whispered weakly. "I am going to my cabin."

She walked to the door, her head fallen somewhat back as if she had not the strength to support it erectly, and her hand was fumbling before her as though she were feeling her way. Munroe drew farther back in his chair and clenched his hands as she disappeared. He did not see her as she turned from the door, wavered, and then fell sidelong to the ground.

He dropped his gaze and studied the papers before him vaguely. How would Gilson appear? Would it be Newlands? Would it be Newlands so changed that he could not know him? He remembered Georgeson's description and took heart. It must be the man—"Eyes that grow bright and dark all in a moment."

A sudden shadow fell over him, and, when he looked up, he started erect. A black-bearded giant stood in the door, and in his arms he bore the limp figure of Beatrice, her head drooped back from the supporting arm and one hand hanging helplessly toward the floor.

Chapter Sixteen

SHADOWS OF PRISON BARS

In a thousand years Munroe would not have recognized that lean and hardened face with the corded column of the throat below. It was the eyes that held him, terribly lighted, and the lips, compressed until they seemed to smile. As Munroe stared, he could see the man's hands tighten upon the body of Beatrice, gathering her closer.

"Wait here," said a voice that Munroe hardly knew. "I am coming back in a moment. I will talk to you then, Munroe!"

He turned and strode from the door and up the hill to the other cabin a short distance away, thrust open the door with his foot, and laid Beatrice on the bed within. He would have turned away to look for some water, but he could not draw his eyes from the white face before him. He gazed at her long and steadfastly, watching the faint rise and fall of her breast, the delicate curve of the throat, the pale, parted lips, and the faint violet penciling of weariness under her fallen eyelids. As he watched, the sorrow, the regret, the vain yearning which had lain locked in his heart all those days, the passion that he had striven to spend in the labors of the mine, the hopelessness that had lain down with him to sleep—all this burst loose and swept him away in a great passion of tenderness and grief. And he was laboring to give this woman to another man, spending his heart and his strength like water to ensure her happiness with another man.

He turned away now and clutched his face with those great, labor-seared hands, and into his mind came the little phrase that had haunted him since that hour when he had taken the request of Crawford upon his shoulders. It chanted now like a little voice: *It is better for her. It is better for her.*

But when he turned back and looked at her again, the big heart swelled to bursting, and a thin, thrusting pain irked him. She lay so coldly beautiful. Her hand thrown out, palm up, against the coverlet seemed to him like the whole body of a woman, fashioned very fair and slender, curving and tremulously dear. There was no harm in touching that hand.

He pressed it over his hot eyes, and the touch was like a benediction. He kissed the cold, soft hollow and every petal fingertip, one by one. The delicate touch of her flesh maddened him, passed from the hot pressure of his questing lips through his whole body—a current of wine in his blood.

He remembered on an evening long ago—age-old that evening seemed—how the sunset had fallen on her throat and filled that hollow like a cup of fairy gold. He kissed that hollow, kissed the shadowed eyes, and the white sorrow of the lips. At that she moaned, and he could feel her breathing against him. At once he started up and stood away, and, as she opened her eyes, she saw him standing, his cap crushed in his hand and his eyes hotly upon her.

Perhaps the memory of those hands upon her still lingered in her conscious mind. Perhaps the kisses still were hot upon her lips, for, as she raised herself wearily upon one arm and faced him, her face was tinted faintly and something of wonder looked on him from her eyes.

She could not remember clearly. She only knew that the instant before—or perhaps it had been hours before—a blackness had come upon her as she stepped from the cabin, and through the mists came the figure of Gilson up the hill. She had felt, too, some great strength raise her in cradling arms, and then there was nothingness until she woke from one dream to another with a sense of a thousand passionate caresses still burning her.

He had turned somewhat away and stood with his hands clenched tightly behind him and his head bowed between the bulging shoulders. The sight of that posture startled her back to full consciousness. There was something ominously familiar about it. She strove to think back into the past, but, as he turned the lean and bearded face toward her again, her memory failed her, and only the wonder remained— wonder—and a sense of content in the power of this man.

Then as she remembered Gurney who had been in the cabin below, remembered the cause for which she had summoned Gilson, she started up a little on the bed, and before the words would come she pointed down toward the other house.

Newlands did not wait for the speech. "I know," he answered, and she started at the grimness of his voice. "I have seen him."

There was something of despair in his tone, and it shocked her through. Perhaps this stranger, Gurney, with the pale face and the expressionless eyes, might have a power over Gilson. The very thought chilled her with terror. She rose and made a step toward him, and, as she did so, she saw him lurch a little toward her without moving his feet, and she saw at the same time a great effort of control that gathered his strength and drew him back again. He stepped to the door.

"I have seen him, and I am going back to him," he said, and she saw a flush of rage go up his face. "I am going now." The door swung open, the big form blocked out the light, and then stepped beyond. The door closed again.

Beatrice stood for a long time in the center of the room. One hand still lay against her breast, and the other was half outstretched as if she were about to speak to the blank wall.

Newlands strode rapidly down the hill. What he would do when he met Munroe he did not dream. He only knew his blind rage. As he stumbled into the room again, he found Munroe tilted back in his chair lighting another of his inevitable cigarettes. He felt the anger burn strangely lower, but he spoke out while it lasted.

"Munroe," he said, "if you have touched her, if you have hurt her in any way, I'll dig your heart out with my bare hands."

Munroe raised his eyes slowly from the cigarette, and lowered them again with a smile.

"Damn you!" cried Newlands fiercely, "why are you here? Isn't the city large enough for the little hells you arrange? Why in God's name have you come here?"

Munroe raised his eyes again, but this time they did not fall. "One hundred thousand dollars." He sighed.

Newlands moved a step back and rested one hand against the wall. The strength seemed to have gone from him. He folded his arms, and Munroe saw that where the hand fell on the other arm it was gripping deep.

"It was really naughty of you to run away like that," continued Munroe gently. "So peevish to leave poor Jimmy Munroe down in the large and lonely city without a word of you. How could I tell whether you were alive or dead?"

"I'm not alive to you now, Munroe," said Newlands. "How did you discover me here?"

"Your talkative friend Benedict told me all about it. You shouldn't leave your affairs in the hands of such noisy people, really."

"Don't lie," said Newlands coldly. "Benedict would cut out his tongue before he would speak to you. How did you find out?"

"Well, then," sighed Munroe, "if you must know, I'll admit that I overheard him when you telephoned. The light on the gentle cut-throat's face told me that you must be on the other end of the wire. Of course, the rest was easy."

"What a snake you are, Jimmy," murmured Newlands. "What a slimy, creeping snake."

Up to this point Munroe felt that he was getting on badly. The time had certainly come when he must play all his cards, one after another, or he would lose out. "Even a snake must live, Billy," he said. "And I'm only a poor, honest fellow who is trying hard to make his way in the world. Really, the only reason I came up here was to collect an honest . . . debt."

Newlands turned somewhat and met his eye fiercely. "Debt?"

"Exactly. Twenty-five thousand dollars for half an hour's work as a man of God. It was really worth it, don't you think? Because our dear friend Crawford really seems to appreciate her, eh?"

The madness came again in Newlands's eyes, but it passed and left his face lined but calm. "Yes," he answered, "I think he will make her happy."

Munroe watched him with a puzzled frown. That Newlands had changed greatly he had appreciated at the first glance, but that he had become capable of such deep and careful acting was beyond credence.

"I've always admitted that you're a great man, Billy," he said, "but I'm afraid that you're getting a little too great for me to follow you. Unbend, m'lord. Crack the safe. Let me in on the dark secret. In other words, what's the game?"

"There is no game," said Newlands.

Munroe chuckled softly. "One hundred thousand dollars," he whispered. "Oh, Billy, you are more than great. At this moment you are actually sublime. One hundred thousand dollars and yet you don't call it a game. You should be on Wall Street with your abilities. You can't keep me on the hook. Billy, I'm bound to wriggle off pretty soon. Come, now, be a nice boy and tell what it's all about. I can really understand almost everything except the beard."

"The beard," Newlands responded, "is just the beginning of a lot of things you can never understand, Jimmy."

"Especially the part about the game that isn't a game, eh?"

"Exactly."

"Well, I suppose it would be a waste of my time to guess. So we'll cut the matter short. I want the twenty-five thousand, Billy."

Newlands started. "I haven't that much money."

Munroe laughed almost frankly. He was enjoying the sport more than he had expected. "One hundred thousand dollars." he repeated, and smiled. "Are you getting parsimonious in your old age, Billy?"

Newlands stared at him mutely. "I will never touch that money, Jimmy," he said at last.

Munroe rose and commenced to walk up and down the room. "I can't understand," he answered. "I don't see what the opening is. I can't see." He turned about and studied Newlands again, slowly shaking his head. "I won't believe you're trying to double-cross me, Billy," he said, "for I know you too well. What is it? Is the money sacred?" He started as a new and strange idea came to him, and then stepped closer to Newlands and spoke in his very face.

"By all the gods, Billy," he said, and he began to smile slowly as the solution of the problem came to him. "You have fallen in love with the girl! Bachelor Billy Newlands!" He noticed Newlands wince, and saw a perceptible pallor on his face, but the big fellow did not speak. Munroe sat down suddenly in a chair and wiped his forehead. "It can't be," he muttered. "This is all a bad dream. And yet, by God, it must be a fact. Billy, you have fallen in love with the girl, and now you're working to secure a fortune for the man who will marry her! If I saw the thing staged, I would laugh, but this is real life."

"And the answer?" queried Newlands, speaking for the first time in some moments.

"One hundred thousand dollars," Munroe responded, as if he had not heard, but he was thinking hard and fast. He whirled with a sudden hardening of the face. "The only way you can talk to me is through a bank book, Newlands," he stated.

"Otherwise?"

"Otherwise, you go up, Billy," he answered. "As sure as some fools are that there's a God in heaven, that's just how sure I am that you'll go up. I know I'll go with you, but I'm damned if I wouldn't rather spend fifteen years in jail than be beaten out of twenty-five thousand dollars by a fool's conscience. That's final."

He had made Newlands shrink before, but now he was astonished to see him smile a little grimly.

"Very well," Newlands said, "then that settles it."

Munroe watched him almost with awe. Verily he was not talking with the old Billy Newlands. But more thoughts were occurring to him.

"But you don't see the point," he continued slowly. "You are very far away from the point, Billy. It doesn't matter so much about you, but what will happen to the girl? Can you see Crawford's face when he hears that this future wife is to be dragged through all the scandals of low life? Can you read his mind when he learns that she has been a boarder at *Madame* Fenwick's? I can. It is all as clear as a picture."

Newlands stepped back a little toward the wall, and his lips stiffened. "Jimmy," he said, and an almost imploring note crept into his voice, "you won't do that. You can't do that!"

"Can't I?" Munroe grinned. "You don't know me, Billy. You ought to know better than that, though. Just slant your eye back over my past as you know it . . . and there's a lot of chapters you've never seen. When you remember all these things, do you still think I'd stop?"

Newlands made a clumsy gesture, and his hand fell back against his side.

"More than that," said Munroe. "Far more than that. The story just begins to open up." He rose excitedly and laughed. "When I peach on you, you're taken away from the mine. That's obvious. Then what happens? All these laborers you've been whipping and coaxing to work rise up and storm the works, beat it, leave Crawford to work his mine with his own hands. And Crawford in an invalid chair . . . he's lost. All your work to save him is lost . . . just as you're about to win for him. He's a failure, the laughingstock of every mining engineer in the country. He's a failure forever, and yet he's the man with whom Beatrice has to live the rest of her life. I tell you. . . ."

He broke off suddenly and leaped away, but the wall stopped his retreat, and he cowered against it. For Newlands leaned above him with the great hands tensed and trembling an inch from Munroe's throat. Jimmy looked into that convulsed face and knew that the balance of a scruple would decide his life or death. Then, just as quickly, Newlands straightened, turned away, and flung both hands over his head.

"Why can't I do it?" he groaned. "My God, why can't I end it all now? A little pressure of my hands and you'd be done for, Munroe, and I could throw your body out to the dogs and no one the wiser. Why can't I do it?"

Munroe stepped away from the wall and loosened his collar somewhat. "Never a fear of that, Billy," he said with a fairly even voice, although he was still pale. "I'm as safe in your hands as a babe in the cradle. If I were taller, it might be different, but as things are, some of your absurd ideas about the sporting chance stand in the way. That's what keeps you from being efficient. Too many ideas, Billy . . . far too many ideas."

Newlands had sunk into a chair and sat now with his chin in his hand and his eyes staring straight before him. It reminded Munroe oddly enough of Crawford's attitude the day before, but the grief and uncertainty of Crawford appeared as nothing in the face of this agony.

"Think how simple it is," went on Munroe soothingly. "You have the pocketbook control of the money. All you have to do is to make out a check and pass it to me and then I pass out of your life and the life of Beatrice, if you will. Isn't it as plain as reading in a book, eh?"

"What a hellhound you are, Munroe," whispered Newlands. "What a veritable devil!"

"Right," said Munroe. "And believe me, Billy, as a devil I can come a lot nearer to being letter-perfect than you ever can in the rôle of a saint. Man, don't you see you are playing a part you can never play to a finish? Don't you see that, if you persist, you'll bring ruin to both yourself and the girl? Self-sacrifice is all right in books, Newlands, but it doesn't do in real life. Now look here, on the one hand you can be a saintly fool and ruin everybody. On the other hand, you can be a reasonable man and make everybody happy. Why, man, do you suppose the girl will miss the twenty-five thousand dollars when she has Crawford and a mine that will bring him hundreds of thousands, probably?"

Newlands brushed his forehead with a trembling hand.

"And there's a better way out than this," Munroe said. "There's a way that puts all the cards in the pack into your hand. You can have everything, if you will. Don't sit there with that burned look, man. Will you listen to me?"

"Say it," said Newlands. "I'll listen. God help me, there's nothing else I can do."

Chapter Seventeen

SOFT-SPOKEN, LYING WORDS

t was very clear to Munroe that Newlands had given up for he moment, and yet he was still at a loss as to the best way in which to push his advantage. He had thought at first that he might force Newlands into signing over to him twenty-five thousand upon which they had agreed before, but he saw plainly that Newlands would never touch Beatrice's money so long as she belonged to another man. He stepped somewhat closer and studied Newlands gravely.

"There is one move left to you," he said, "and that is to go back and claim her as your wife after you have wrecked the prospects of this man Crawford."

Newlands lifted his head slowly and gazed blankly at Munroe as if he could not understand. Munroe repeated his words, counting them out with lifted forefinger like a mother teaching a child.

"The one thing you want in your life is Beatrice," Munroe stated, "and, if you're half a man, you will get her."

Newlands made a vague gesture of repulsion and shook his head in renunciation. Munroe came still nearer. It took courage to do what he was about to do, but he saw that the spirit of Newlands was at the lowest ebb. He put one hand under Newlands's chin, and the other hand on his forehead, and lifted. The head rolled heavily and limply back upon the big shoulders, and Munroe found himself staring into two lifeless eyes.

"If you want her," said Munroe, "you can have her. Do you understand?"

There was no answering light in the night-dark eyes.

"It is all as simple as child's play," Munroe went on rapidly, "if you really want her. Will you tell me that? By God, you don't need to tell me. You are hungry for her, man. What? Didn't I see you stand there in the door a moment ago with your hands tightening around her body? Wouldn't you give half the world for the right to see her again?"

The big head rolled forward and down again, and Newlands groaned. But Munroe felt that the first step was won to him. Newlands was roused at last.

"Martyrs," went on Munroe, "have always made interesting history. As a fact in everyday life, they're a damned bore. You'll see the point of that, Newlands. Why, my dear boy, are you a fool to stay up here and tear your heart in two in order to give Beatrice to Crawford? Do you think she would be happy with him?"

Newlands started violently in his chair, and then rose. "Jimmy," he whispered, "talk very slowly now. Do you mean to say that she doesn't love him?"

Munroe threw back his head and laughed aloud, as much to assure himself as to impress Newlands.

"Why, you addle-pated ass!" he cried. "Do you think she could really love a cold-blooded fish like Crawford? All that man is vitally interested in is his business. What she wants is a man, a strong man, a man who makes and breaks things . . . a man like you, Billy."

Newlands ground a clenched fist slowly back over his head and brought it to a halt, straining behind his neck. "But she has lived with him . . . she is living with him now," he muttered.

Again Munroe laughed. "As an observer of life and human nature, Billy," he said coldly, "you belong in a class by yourself, somewhere below the Kindergarten. Why, man, don't you see that she only stays with Crawford to take care of him? Don't you see that she only stays here as his wife so as to be able to be safe among those roughneck miners? Haven't you observed that she lives in a house by herself? Does that look like love?"

He waited a moment and saw the thought sink slowly into Newlands's consciousness, and then answering light on his face.

"It is mere friendship," went on Munroe. "She has saved his life, and he's grateful to her. She likes him as a friend. That's the sum total of the affair. They feel that they are necessary to each other. What? Haven't I lived here in the cabin with Crawford for days and days? Haven't I watched them every moment of the day and night?"

"Jimmy," Newlands said, "I won't ask you to swear any oaths, because I know you haven't any soul left in your rotten body, but will you give me your hand with all the manhood that's in you and repeat what you've said?"

Perhaps there was an instant of hesitation in Munroe, but he was thinking too rapidly to make it a long delay. His hand shot out and gripped Newlands's, and he winced under the return pressure.

"I believe every word I have just told you about the relations between those two," he said. "I give you my hand as man to man on it, Billy."

Newlands drew a great breath and released the hand.

"But," Munroe went on eagerly, "you haven't seen clear through to the end yet. I have said that she doesn't love him yet, and she doesn't. But she likes him a lot, and he wants her. If things go on drifting like this, don't you understand that they will marry in the end?" He saw Newlands wince. "You poor blockhead," he went on bitterly, "do you think that marriages are made for wild love only? Rot! These two will marry simply because they've got used to each other. Here you are working your heart out in the mine, making a damned martyr of yourself. In the end you will win out for him. You'll make him a millionaire several times over from the look of things. He goes to Beatrice and puts at her feet the money Newlands has made for him. He offers it to her and asks if she could be happy with him. 'Well,' she says, drifting her hand through a thousand pounds of gold, 'I think we might make a pair of it. Are you going to reward Gilson, Steven, dear?' 'Bah!' says dear Steven. 'He's simply a rough miner. I'll send him a flask of whisky for a reward.' 'Quite right,' says Beatrice; 'when do we move to Paris, Steven, love?' And there you are! Nice picture, Billy, isn't it? Are you going to play into their hands like that?"

"By God!" Newlands cried. "I'll see Crawford in hell first!"

Munroe sighed and drew forth a cigarette, which he lighted with infinite content. "The first flash of intelligence, Billy," he said. "We will have to advance you out of the Kindergarten class."

"You are sure she doesn't love him?" Newlands repeated half to himself, and then he went on answering his own question: "Bah! How can she love him? He is nothing but a mind. She is meant for the real passion of a real man. Munroe, I tell you I begin to feel that there is still a hope for me!"

"Only in one way," Munroe assured him, "only in one way do you get inside the door. Break Crawford, sink him like a rotten hulk. Then the rats will leave the sinking ship. They always do, Billy, and, when Beatrice leaves, you step in and take her."

"You underrate her, Jimmy," Newlands said, shaking his head. "She would not leave him then. She wouldn't leave him when he's down and out."

"Don't be an ass," Munroe said with some disgust. "Don't you see that, if he's broke and sinking, he'll refuse to exercise any claim over her? Do you suppose that he'd marry her when he's a failure? No, he's not built that way."

"But am I?" Newlands questioned. "Am I built so as to wreck the hopes of Crawford now?"

"Well," said Munroe, "at least there is no doubt that you could wreck them if you wished to. Eh?" He dared not let his anxiety enter into his voice.

Newlands made a vague gesture of assent. "If I stop driving the men for a single day," he said, "they would drop their tools and walk out. They're sick of the Victory Mine." Newlands's face was suddenly lined and grim.

"Well?" said Munroe.

"I can't do it," Newlands muttered. "I can't double-cross this man. I have saved him once already. I have saved him almost every day since the first I was here. Can I double-cross him now? Jimmy, it can't be done!"

Munroe tossed the cigarette away and smashed his fist into the hollow of his hand. "Then you take the results, Billy, my boy. I've played at the square deal with you till I'm sick of it all. I tell you, if you back out on this, you may as well order your suit of stripes, because you're going to have a long rest in San Quentin, Billy . . . a very long rest. I think it's fifteen years for this sort of thing, eh? I go with you, but only for half as long. I'm merely an accessory in the game, Billy. I'm merely the poor tool you bullied into the job. Oh, I'll get off easily enough, but Bachelor Billy Newlands will be soaked the limit by any judge in California. A society rake that took advantage of an innocent girl. It makes fine meat for the papers, eh?"

"You would do it, Munroe," Newlands observed, with a vague sort of wonder, as if all his passion had been burned out. "I really think you would do it."

"Right," snapped Munroe. "You know I would. At the same time when you step out of this mine, Crawford goes to wreck just as badly as if you had double-crossed him. Do you get that point?"

Newlands sank back into his chair.

"And the other way," went on Munroe, growing more and more enthusiastic as he drew his picture, "the mine breaks up, and who emerges as the hero of the picture? Why, no one but Jim Gilson, the man who accomplished the impossible, the man who held the miners at their work for days and days. Then this Jim Gilson goes to Beatrice, goes to her after she has talked with Crawford and they have agreed that all thoughts of matrimony will have to be postponed. I say Jim Gilson, the hero, goes to her and plants himself in front of her and says . . . 'Beatrice, I am Newlands. I have been here all this time, trying to serve your happiness. But I want you too much. I can't stay away from you. Beatrice, I want you as my wife!' What will she do? Bah! What would any woman do when she discovers that an honest-to-God hero is her very own husband who has been trying to make a martyr of his foolish self for her sake? Why, man, she will simply fall into your arms and weep . . . and there you are. For all this time she hasn't an idea that you are anything other than her real husband."

"If I play the man's part," Newlands said, pondering over each word as if it required separate thought, "you step in and spoil four lives . . . hers, Crawford's, yours, and mine. If I play the crooked game, you stay out, Beatrice and I are happy . . .

for, by God, I know I could make her happy . . . and the scapegoat is one man . . . Crawford!"

"Right," said Munroe, "and I'll help. Tell Crawford that you'd like to have me down in the mine. I'll say that I knew you years ago and would like to be with you. He'll let me go. Once in the mine, I'll start dissension. I'll slip a word in the ears of a few of the half-intelligent men. In the meantime, you hold back on your authority. Give them free rein for a day or so. Why, we'll have them all up in arms and walking out of the mine within seventy-two hours."

"And then?" Newlands asked.

"And when you have the lady you love"—Munroe smiled, waving an airy hand—"then you simply slip me a check for twenty-five thousand . . . and the game is done. I think I've done twenty-five thousand dollars' worth of work for it already."

Newlands clutched his hands behind him and glowered down at Munroe.

"I am like a child," he said with a fiercely controlled voice, "like a child in your hands now, Munroe. What you say seems to go just now. But the time may come when you'll walk in my dust, understand? Anyway, I'm not going to sneak behind you like a dog in the dark. I'm telling you now. If I see another way open to me, I'm going to use it, understand?"

"Sure," said Munroe, "if you can beat me out in this game, you're welcome, Billy. I have never held malice against superior brains."

"I'm going to get out of here," Newlands growled after a slight pause. "But what a hound you are, Munroe . . . what a heartless, soft-footed hound you are."

From the window of her cabin, Beatrice watched them walk down the hill side by side, and her heart sank as she noted them.

For Munroe walked with his head turned toward his companion. But Gilson strode with his head dropped between his bulging shoulders.

They were nearly at the bottom of the slope when she saw the pair come to an abrupt halt. Munroe turned and faced Gilson squarely. Finally Gilson threw a clenched hand above his head and straightened as if he had come to a violent resolution, and afterward the pair walked on together, but this time they were arm-in-arm.

Chapter Eighteen

BREWERS OF MUTINY

That night after supper when Jim Donnelly read off the names of the lucky men who had received mail, Newlands was astonished to hear "Jim Gilson" called out. He took the envelope with great curiosity and recognized at once the careful handwriting of Benedict. He waited until he reached the seclusion of his bed in the bunkhouse before he opened the letter and read the following:

Dear Mr. Newlands,

I have waited for several days before I write this. I could hardly make up my mind about it. Now I know that I must send you a warning.

When you telephoned to me, I did not know that Mr. Munroe was within hearing distance, but, when I turned from the telephone, I saw him standing in the hall. He had heard everything, and said he was going to see you. By this time he may be there.

If he is there, I wish you would tell me. It is very important.

This is the time to say other things, also.

When you first found me, I was half starved and lying in the street where I had fallen. You carried me home and made me a man again. This I have not forgotten. For many years ago I was a gentleman, and I still have some thoughts of which a gentleman would not be ashamed.

In those days long ago I once knew Mr. Munroe. At that time he did me a great wrong. This I have not forgotten, for I am a Spaniard, and a Spanish gentleman does not forget either good or evil.

I recognized Munroe when I met him at your house. He did not know me, for I have changed, but before he left the house to find you, I think he had begun to suspect who I am. Therefore, he will be on his guard against me.

But if Munroe is with you, he is not there for your good. He has never brought good to anyone. Therefore, I hope you will be wary with him.

Furthermore, please let me know of his coming. Then I will come, also. I am eager to see him now. What he has done in my past has been like a red writing that can only be rubbed out with more red. I have not forgotten any of these things. If he troubles you now, it shall make me gladder to see him.

Pedro Benedict

It was a strange letter to Newlands. He had often guessed that Benedict was not a servant by birth, but the man's past had always been a closed book to him. Now he thought over many little things, and many signs of Benedict's steady devotion during the long years of his service. The riddle began to clear in his mind. He found paper and ink and wrote to his valet briefly:

My Dear Benedict,
Munroe is here, but you must not come. You could not possibly live here, even for a short time. No one is

allowed to come near the mine except the men who labor in it.

You can be sure that I will watch Munroe and be on my guard against him. I can take care of myself without your help, though I appreciate your warning.

As for your past, Benedict, I am not in the least curious. Perhaps Munroe has injured you, but you will have to try to forget it, at least for a while.

And don't think that you owe me any debt that should be repaid at the expense of Munroe. If I started by doing you some sort of kindness, you have long ago repaid it with your service. I assure you that the score is quite clear between us.

William Newlands

Yet he felt far more keenly about the matter than he let it appear in his letter. He wondered deeply in what way Benedict had been entangled with Munroe in the past.

Now it came back to him. As he had laid in his bed that morning, long ago, when Munroe had come into his room, he had glanced into the mirror and seen Benedict's face reflected there, scowling hatefully as the gambler came in. It had startled him at the time, such terrible, such silent malevolence. Then, again, he recalled little fleeting impressions of Benedict watching Munroe from the corner of his eye with a palpable hatred. He had put it down at the time to some blind prejudice on the part of the little Spaniard. It grew into a greater significance now.

But he shrugged the matter from his mind. Other affairs claimed his attention, and they were affairs to which he must give himself wholly. He did not pause for self-analysis. If he were doing evil, it seemed a predestined evil from which there was no escape, and the result of the crime was a prize for which he would have sold his soul to hell a thousand times—Beatrice. For she stayed with him in all hours, and the picture of her gestures, the little pauses and catches of her breath, the light murmur of her laugh, these things slept with him at night and met him like a smile in the morning.

The first part of their plans went through easily enough. When Crawford heard of Gilson's request to have Munroe in the mine, he acquiesced with some reluctance. He still needed Munroe to work at the accounts, but he desired to please Gilson, and finally decided to let Munroe spend half his time in the mine, working there one day and at his accounts the next.

Once there, Munroe acted his part with masterly skill. Sometimes Newlands would see him in the center of a group of workers in some drift, the men standing around him with their tools idle in their hands.

When Newlands came up, the men met him with black looks and went on their way with manifest reluctance. In the bunkhouse, at night, he would see Munroe in the midst of the largest circle, always telling some tale that enraptured his listeners. They were always stories laid in the heart of the city, adventures with policemen, encounters with bartenders. Frequently he would pause to describe some delectable drink that he had had to instruct some bartender how to mix. And the miners listened with fixed smiles and wondering eyes. These tales were to them like the call of the trumpet to the soldier.

Afterward, when they commenced to grumble against their restricted life at the mine, Munroe did not mix in the arguments. When they dwelt upon Crawford's coldness, he nodded his head knowingly. When they spoke of the possibility of uncovering a rich strike in the Victory, he went so far as to laugh aloud. It was a hoodoo mine, he suggested, and the phrase went the rounds in the course of a single evening. A hoodoo mine that would bring no luck to anyone working in it, and there was no gold there except fool's gold.

But with this trouble brooding, it was impossible that some notice of it should not come to headquarters. Georgeson himself made the first objection to Newlands.

It was after lunch in the mess hall one day that he approached Newlands and asked to speak apart with him for a few moments. Newlands sensed the discussion that was coming and saw no way to avoid it. He led Georgeson to one corner of the mess hall and waited for the comment.

"Jim" he said to Newlands, "I have a hunch that you'll think I'm butting in on your affairs. But something has been bothering me a lot the last two days, an' I want to talk to you about it."

"Fire away, old-timer," Newlands said. "Let's hear it!"

"Well," said Georgeson, "all I've got to say an' all I've got to complain of will fit nice and easy in one word . . . Gurney, this new man Jim Gurney."

"What's the matter?" queried Newlands.

"Say," evaded Georgeson, "is he a friend of yours, because if he is, I'm through an' got nothing to say."

"Just an acquaintance," Newlands assured him. "I used to know him pretty well, and that's how he got the job down here."

Georgeson sighed with relief and knitted his forehead to recall everything he had to say. "It's rather hard to get all this straight," he started at last, "but the long and short of it is that I don't like the cut of this new guy . . . not a bit."

"No?" Newlands said casually.

"Not a damned bit!" Georgeson vowed. "I wish he was about a hundred miles away from this here mine. Look at him now!"

They turned and looked at Munroe, who sat among a group of pipe-smoking miners. Everyone in the group was leaning closer and closer toward Munroe as he talked.

"You see that?" Georgeson asked angrily.

"Sure I do," Newlands said, "he's over there talking with a lot of the boys. What of it?"

"What of it?" Georgeson repeated. "Say, Gilson, you sure surprise me a lot. Don't you know the way that guy has been talking for the last few days . . . ever since he got into the mine?"

"How?"

"Handing out the barroom talk until all the boys are dry all the way down their throats. And he has a lot of talk about things the boys are all interested in. He can tell them all the latest dope on the prize fights. He makes them see the sawdust on the floor, I tell you. He's simply driving the boys crazy. He's making them want to go to town terribly bad, and God knows they wanted to go bad enough before he came."

"Hmm," Newlands muttered, striving desperately for something to say and finding nothing.

"Oh, it's something worth grunting over," urged Georgeson. "I thought you were noticing it and getting ready with something up your sleeve to play on this new guy. I never dreamed that you were letting things drift. I tell you that if you wait too long, there'll be nothing that can stop the boys when they break loose. Once before you were able to stop them when they got started, but I doubt whether even you and I could stop them together now. They are losing all faith in the mine. Every time anyone talks about the big vein that Crawford is trying to strike, this guy Gurney sits back and laughs, and then the boys get silent and thoughtful. I tell you he's getting them to the point where they will do anything, and, when they start, God help anyone who tries to stand in their way."

"This sounds like queer talk to me," Newlands said gravely, "and I'll keep a close eye on our friend Gurney. Don't take it too seriously, though, Georgeson. I've watched the men growl ever since I came to the mine. It's just a habit with them."

Georgeson rubbed his chin meditatively with a huge, half-clenched fist. "Do you know, Jim," he said at last, "if I hadn't seen you stand up and make the whole gang back down once before, I'd be thinkin' now that you was just letting things drift for the sake of the excitement that's comin', but, believe me, when the bust does come, you'll wish the whole army was hangin' around to help you."

"All right!" Newlands laughed. "Maybe you have the dope, but I want to see it for myself before I do anything with Gurney. In the meantime, don't go around looking like a thundercloud. Just leave this thing to me."

Chapter Nineteen

JACK DONNELLY SMELLS TROUBLE

It had been a cheerful supper at the cabin. The brown array of fried trout had vanished one by one, and there were vast inroads on the potatoes that Beatrice had prepared *au gratin* with infinite care, so that Crawford pronounced them the last word in fine cookery. Now he sat back with his black coffee poised on the arm of his chair and his cigar in his left hand. He waved it in time with the song of Beatrice:

"Skeeters am a-hummin' 'round the watermelon vine. . . ."

He joined in desperately on the next to the last line, his voice creaking on a high note. They stopped singing and laughed together.

"And you've spoiled my perfectly good song." Beatrice smiled.

"I have to do something," he said. "Something to entertain you."

"Then get up and walk around the room," Beatrice coaxed.

He stared at her a moment incredulously. "Do you think I might try?" he said eagerly.

"Yes," she said, studying him with her head tilted to one side, "I think you might. You have no idea how rosy and healthy you look tonight."

He tossed the blanket that was spread over him and, with her assistance, rose carefully to his feet. Then, leaning on her shoulder, he began a slow progress around the room. At the table he stopped a moment to rest, and the pressure of his arm around her shoulders, drawing her to him, made her flush.

"The pauses"—grinned Crawford—"are the most interesting moments of this promenade. By Jove! I feel as if I could run a mile uphill."

But the strain had begun to tell on him, and he made his way back to the chair with his arm around her. It was a proud moment for her, this test of his strength, and she tasted to the full all the fruits of victory—victory over death and the prostration that had held this man so long. And the pride showed in her eyes and in her smile as her hand moved across his hair with the touch of possession.

"Do you realize what it means when I can walk?" he asked.

"Of course," she said. "It means that you are nearly well."

"More than that," he insisted. "It has been well enough for us to stay apart while I was sick and needed some care day and night, but when I am strong and walking around . . . what will people think with you living in one cabin and I in another . . . a queer married pair, eh, Beatrice?"

She started to rise.

"Don't go," he protested. "I can say what I have to say a lot better with you close to me. Beatrice, haven't things come to the breaking point at last? Can we go any further this way?"

"There can't be any other way for us," she said firmly, but her head was turned for fear of meeting his eyes.

"Never any other way?" he persisted.

She was silent.

"There is always some way out," he went on. "There is some fine way for us, Beatrice, isn't there? I know that there is something holding you back. I gathered it clearly enough that afternoon when Gurney brought out his damned cards. And for a while I had all sorts of unworthy thoughts and wild conjectures, but that has all passed over. I love you so much, Beatrice, so bitterly much. Can't you see it?"

"Love?" she said slowly, as if she hardly understood what he had said. "Love?"

She started suddenly erect and away from him. Was this love? This faintly pressing arm, this brotherly tenderness? Into her mind came two strange memories.

The first was Newlands as he had waited for her at the bottom of the stairs after the wedding. The second was far different: the moment when she awoke on her bed in the other cabin with a dream-like memory of stern-lipped kisses still tingling in her mouth and throat, and then she had looked up and seen the bowed figure of Gilson, black-bearded, his eyes buried deep under frowning brows. She could recall every detail of that strong and tortured figure, even the hands gripping whitely on his crushed hat. She covered her face with both hands and shuddered slightly, standing for a long moment with her thoughts.

She turned swiftly and went to Crawford where he sat, leaning forward in his chair. She caught his hands in her tensed fingers and brought them together beneath his chin, forcing his head back slowly until she was looking directly down in his face. He knew that he was being weighed and tested in that moment, but he met her searching eyes fairly enough, as suddenly she dropped his hands and sank down again on the arm of the chair. She seemed weary all at once, or outworn with the passion of those memories. She buried her face in the crook of her arm, where it rested against the back of the chair and very near Crawford's head.

"I won't talk much more about it if it troubles you so,

dear," he said gently, "but at least you will tell me that it is all right? That when the day comes I may send for a minister?"

A loud knock came at the door, and, as Beatrice rose and stepped away, the door opened upon Donnelly. Crawford bit his lips to keep back the expression of his anger.

" 'Evening," said Donnelly. "Hope you'll excuse me for comin' in here sudden this way, but I've got something I think you ought to hear, Mister Crawford."

"Fire away, Jack," Crawford said somewhat wearily. "What's your trouble now?"

Donnelly's eyes shifted uncertainly from one object to another in the room, and he flushed. Obviously what he had to say was not an easy matter of expression.

"Sit down, Jack," Beatrice suggested, noticing his embarrassment, "and take your time about talking."

He sighed and sat down gingerly on the edge of a chair. "It bothers me a lot to say this here," he began, "but I'll bat right into the middle of it, an' you can draw your own conclusions."

"Right," Crawford agreed. "Let her go."

"Well," said Donnelly, "it's Gilson."

There was a little cry from Beatrice, but, when Crawford turned his head, she had already gained control of herself.

"Wait a minute, Jack," Crawford said. "Go awfully careful, now. Gilson is a bad man to talk about."

"I wish to God that he was here to listen to what I've got to say," Donnelly stated, "because then maybe he'd be able to explain. I tell you Gilson is losing his grip."

Crawford paled visibly. "The men are getting troublesome again?" he asked.

"They've always been that, damn them," Donnelly spit. "They were too much for me from the first, and the only way Gilson has kept them going has been by hounding them every day . . . he and his lieutenant, Georgeson. Half of the boys are afraid of those two, and the other half keep on because they like him. That's the way Gilson has run the mine when it looked like nobody between here an' hell could do it."

"That's all an old story," Crawford added eagerly. "I know what Gilson has done. The point is what is he doing now?"

"That's it," said Donnelly, straightening in his chair. "He's doing nothing now. Not a thing. He lets the men talk as they please and work as they please. Maybe he's tired out, but he looks a long way from being a tired man. He's just simply changed all at once."

Crawford groaned and leaned back in his chair. "Gilson, too!" he cried. "My God, is there no one in the world who's square and will give a man a man's deal?"

Beatrice stepped a little closer to Donnelly and faced Crawford. Her eyes were angry. "What a strange thing to say, Steven," she said coldly. "I know you are not serious. You cannot doubt Gilson. Hasn't he saved the mine and you before? Why should he change now, unless. . . ." She stopped and blanched. "Jack," she cried fiercely to Donnelly, "has Gilson changed since that new man . . . since Gurney went to the mine?"

Donnelly's eyes widened as he stared back to her. "How did you know that?" he asked.

"It *is* Gurney!" exclaimed Crawford. "Beatrice, I haven't liked that man since he told your fortune that afternoon. There's something of the snake in the fellow. Donnelly, what's Gurney doing to Gilson?"

"God knows," Donnelly said. "If anyone had told me before that there was a man or a woman in the world who could change Gilson, I would have called him a liar to his face. But since Gurney came down, there ain't no doubt of it. Jim

Gilson is changing. I can't put my finger on what Gurney does to Gilson. I know I have seen them together only once, and then they only said half a dozen words. But I know that if any man outside of Gurney acted the way he does, Gilson would break his neck."

Crawford covered his face with his hands and gritted his teeth.

"Gurney goes around and talks with the boys and makes them think about good times outside the mine," went on Donnelly. "He's full of stories about barrooms and drinks and drunks, until every man of the lot gets a thirst that's worse than a sand heap. Then when anyone says something about the big strike which may be made in the Victory, Gurney just sits there and laughs."

"And Gilson lets him do this?"

"He doesn't seem to see it or hear it," Donnelly said, "and I think he doesn't want to."

"Then tell Gilson to get rid of this man Gurney. Send him back here to the cabin, and I'll keep an eye on him if I have to keep him tied hand and foot."

"There ain't no use in that, I'm thinking," Donnelly said. "I think the men have got their minds made up already. They don't even listen to Gilson any more, and they give him black looks when he comes near them. I know what it is. I used to get the same sort when I was boss. They're as bad as a knife in the back."

"There's some way out of it," Beatrice interjected. "I still can't believe that Gilson could go wrong. There must be some mistake there. Steven, he practically saved your life! Gurney is the man. But surely the men can be held together. Steven, there are only ten days left to the lease."

"Only ten days," groaned Crawford. "If I can only keep the boys together until then, I know this vein they're on will open up. I know it."

"Jack," Beatrice said desperately, "they surely can be held for ten days longer?"

Donnelly raised his hand in a vague gesture and let it drop back heavily on his knee. "Might as well be ten years," he said. "I don't want to hang around as any croaker. I'm only saying what I think is the truth. You've got to know. Maybe there's something you can think of to do to wake up Gilson. There's the ghost of a show that he could straighten up again. If they once get started, not even Gilson can stop them."

"There's only one way of getting at him," Crawford said, controlling his emotion, although his face was white. "We must work on him through Gurney. Gurney has done this thing. He has some power on Gilson."

"Must have," said Donnelly.

"Tell Gilson that I want to see him," Crawford stated.

"I'll lay you odds that he won't come, or else he'll put it off till tomorrow morning," Donnelly responded. "I've got it figured out that tomorrow morning is about the time they'll break, and Gilson won't be on the stage when the hell starts."

"Tell him I wish to see him tonight, at any rate," Crawford said.

Donnelly rose and walked to the door. "Georgeson is still pulling hard for you," he said as he opened the door, "but he hasn't got the brain to handle this sort of a job. He's simply a good tool when Gilson is handling him. Otherwise, he's worth nothing. I'll tell Gilson that you want him, but I'll take any bet that you won't see him till tomorrow morning." He stepped into the night and closed the door.

No sooner had it closed than Beatrice ran to it, threw it open, and called after him. She did not wait for him to come back into the room, but stepped outside and let the door fall to behind her.

"Yes?" Donnelly said, coming hastily back up the path.

"Jack," she said, "you must do a favor for me, and it's something you must not mention to anyone. Will you? Of course, you will, Jack. I want you to tell Gurney that I must see him. I'm sure that Gilson will let Gurney go out of the bunkhouse if he wants to, and then tell Gurney to come straight up the hill to my cabin."

"To your cabin, ma'am?" Donnelly said in astonishment.

"Yes, yes," whispered Beatrice. "It is very important. Everything may depend on it."

"I don't understand," Donnelly admitted. "This whole thing beats me. Sure, I'll do what you tell me to."

She saw him turn and fade into the night, and went back slowly to the house. She closed the door with an effort and then leaned against it with her eyes closed wearily.

"I wanted to ask Donnelly a question about Gilson," she explained, "but he didn't know the answer."

Crawford made no reply, but it seemed to him, as he sat staring at the floor that he heard her breath catch in a sob as she closed the door behind her and went into the night.

Chapter Twenty

"THE SPITE OF HELL!"

Donnelly had evidently delivered his message at once at the bunkhouse, for as she stepped to the door of her cabin, she found a shadowy figure waiting for her.

"Gurney?" she queried.

"Yes, Missus Newlands," answered a quiet voice.

She said no more, but opened the door and lighted the lamp within. As she turned, Munroe entered and closed the door softly behind him.

He stood politely attentive and respectful, almost servile in his attitude, with his cap straight down at his side.

As Beatrice surveyed him and noted each detail, the task that had seemed difficult enough before seemed practically impossible now. Even the rough clothes could not change Munroe. The heavy boots, the overalls, the open-throated shirt did not make him a laborer, but simply an actor carefully made up for a part. She sighed, and then pointed to a chair.

He thanked her with a bow, and sat down quietly with his hands folded in his lap and his cap between them. For all the world he seemed to her like a naughty child who had come to be scolded for a fault, but his face denied his demeanor. It seemed to Beatrice that if he had been only a little less meaningless of eye she could use some effective persuasion upon

178

him, but in the face of this unhuman coldness she felt helpless.

"I have done a most unconventional thing in sending for you, Mister Gurney," she began, "asking you to call on me alone in the night."

"Perhaps a little unusual," he said gently, "but I hope nothing more."

She dropped her eyes to her interlaced fingers, and frowned. Evidently the only way with Gurney was to be outright assault. "Your work at the mine has become generally known, Mister Gurney," she said at last.

He raised his eyebrows with polite interest. "Indeed?"

"Thoroughly known . . . yes, uncomfortably thoroughly."

"I am so sorry if I have disturbed anyone," he murmured.

"Will you not be frank with me?"

"Of course, I should be glad to be frank."

"Will you admit that you are making dissension in the mine?"

He looked at her with careful surprise. "I am sure I have misunderstood you," he said.

Her hands parted and clutched again at her sides. "I tell you," she went on, "that everything is obvious except your purpose. We know what you are doing and what you are saying. Even some of your conversations with the miners have been reported to us. All of this is clear, and how you are stirring up the laborers to rise in a mob and break away from the mine. We know all this, Mister Gurney."

"It is very strange that so much should be laid at the door of a new laborer at the mine," he complained.

"I can almost admire you," she said, after a little pause, "for you do it so well. But not quite well enough, Mister Gurney, not nearly well enough. But if you will tell me what you expect to gain by this, perhaps we can talk to a better understanding."

"I assure you," he said, "that I could not discuss that point even if I were quite sure what you mean."

"Then it means simply boundless innuendo and nothing accomplished, Mister Gurney," she said. "But I cannot carry on innuendos. I must be frank and outspoken with you. I will not talk about your purpose or your plans. I will merely tell you exactly what you are doing, and beg you to stop if there is yet time to stop."

Munroe half rose from his chair, and a whimsical smile touched his mouth. "What a Thoroughbred you are," he said softly. "What a wonderful little Thoroughbred you are. If I had known. . . ." He broke off and stared at the window. "What was that?"

She looked at him with wonder. "I heard nothing," she said.

"I thought I did," he puzzled. "Out the window there, or in that direction."

"The wind," she said. "It often makes queer noises. There is never anyone wandering about these mountains at night."

"Suppose," he went on, coming sharply back to the point, "that I have some plans that urge me on to do what you have just charged me with. What then?"

"You see it is so hard for me to talk," she said, "for I am in the dark, and you alone know your own motives. But I feel this . . . I know this from what I have seen, that you have some such power over Mister Gilson as you have over me. You know something of a black period in his past. Is not this so?"

"I have followed the actions of some people rather closely," he admitted.

"And you are using that knowledge to make him a traitor to Mister Crawford and to himself?"

He had somewhat abandoned his reserve, and now he

waved his hand in a gesture which might have been taken for assent.

"Mister Gurney, whatever you expect to gain from this thing, it cannot balance the wrong you are doing." She rose and stepped toward him. "I had thought to bring you here and learn what you are trying to do, but I see that I cannot fight against you. You are too well armored at all points. There is one thing left to me, to beg you for God's sake, and the sake of your own and better nature, not to force this thing through."

"I am sorry," muttered Munroe, and he frowned. "I think I am truly sorry," he repeated, and his eyes went up to meet hers.

It was the first point she had scored, and it gave her courage. "You know so much of my past that I shall not try to hide the truth from you," she said. "I cannot think you are inhuman. Then listen. You have called me Missus Newlands. I bear that name by right. But it was a mistake. It is an episode that has never truly occurred. It was no more than a terrible nightmare or a hideous face that one meets in the night and forgets forever. All that past is dead."

She saw his face harden somewhat.

"And yet you are still Missus Newlands?"

"The marriage shall be annulled as soon as this struggle in the mine is over. Mister Gurney, I am laying my heart bare to you. In the cabin below is the man I expect to marry. His life and his happiness depend upon his success in this mine. If he fails, his life is a failure. I know he will not live to be laughed at. He has set his heart upon this venture. Mister Gurney, you are a man. You must respect the manly thing. You must respect him for the work he has done here."

Munroe shrugged his shoulders, but his chin dropped upon his clenched hand and he frowned at the floor.

She went to him and took his hand in both of hers. "Look up at me," she commanded. He raised his head, and she found herself exploring the gray, meaningless eyes. "There are three lives to which you are fate, Mister Gurney," she said rapidly. "If you win out in this thing you have begun, you spoil Mister Crawford's life beyond repair, and . . . and mine with his. But more than that. Yes, somehow, I feel that more than that is the thing you will do to Jim Gilson. He is a big man, a big-minded man. Someday he will move thousands as he now controls a few scores in the mine. And he has acted strongly and surely here, until you came. It was to him that Mister Crawford owed the last opportunity of opening the mine.

"But now I know surely that, if he yields to you here, he will be broken forever. This is his work to redeem what has been perhaps a misspent life. I cannot tell. I only know that, if you will let him work out his own way, he may yet pull us through and save himself at the same time."

She stood a moment in silence. He studied her face, and she his. She had stirred him more than she had dared to hope. She stepped away a moment to let him make his decision, but, as she did so, her eyes fell upon the window, and she sprang cowering back against the opposite wall with a shrill cry.

"What is it?"

"Out the window. There! There! No, it is gone!"

He turned and followed her pointing finger with his eyes. "Where?"

"It is gone," she said faintly. "It was a man. He was watching you."

"Nonsense," cried Munroe, "you are merely excited! This strain has told too heavily on you. There could not have been a watcher."

"I tell you I saw him!" she panted, "at the window there. A long, narrow, dark face, and his eyes were fixed on your face like a wolf's."

"Narrow and dark!" Munroe hissed, and she saw him pale. "My God!"

He turned swiftly and leaped to the door, jerked it open, and ran into the night, and, as he did so, she saw him fumble at his hip pocket. She crouched and waited for a pistol shot.

But none came, and after some moments the door opened softly again and Munroe appeared with a face deathly pale.

"You found him?" she asked.

"Nothing," he said faintly.

The pistol was still clutched in his hand as if he had forgotten it. Now he remembered suddenly and restored it to his pocket.

"A narrow, foreign-looking face?" he asked, and his voice was unsteady as he spoke.

"Yes, yes!" she said. "But the expression. I have never seen such malignant hate. It must have been one of the miners. Have you some enemy there?"

He laughed somewhat hysterically and loosed his already open collar forcibly. "It was not a miner," he said. "I . . . I think it was an old friend of Gilson's. I have been gone too long already."

"And you have no other answer for me?" she pleaded.

"A moment ago I thought that, after all . . . ," he began, and then stopped.

"Then this thing happened."

He threw back his head suddenly with an almost animal ferocity. "I will not stop!" he shouted, and it seemed almost as if he were speaking for the benefit of someone beyond the wall of the cabin. "I will not stop even if I have to drag ten people to hell with me. I am going to put this thing through. It is war, I tell you, war!"

"An unfair war," she reminded him. "For all the odds are already against us. Oh, if you are a man. . . ."

"Bah," he said with a sudden bitterness. "Odds against you with that black devil on the hunt? I tell you I won't be stopped. Am I a boy to be frightened away from the biggest thing of my life?" He stopped and controlled himself with a great effort as if he were ashamed of having said too much.

"I am sorry to have lost my self-control," he murmured at the door. "And I am equally sorry that your time should have been wasted on me, Missus Newlands. The story is not yet ended. When the time comes. . . ." He waved his hand vaguely and went into the night with a low laugh trailing behind him.

When he came to the bunkhouse, he was still so obviously disturbed that Newlands whispered to him as he passed his bunk.

Munroe stopped and sat on the edge of Newlands's bed. Through the big room came the sound of many heavy-breathing sleepers. The dim light of a single smoky lantern picked out rough tables and chairs and fallen garments with vague touches like a painting of the gloomy Flemish school.

"You saw her?" whispered Newlands.

"I did," replied Munroe in an equally guarded voice.

"And?"

"Nothing but talk."

"She has found out what you are doing?"

"They all know."

"Crawford?"

"Yes. I think that fool Donnelly was up there with them tonight before she sent him for me."

"And they suspect me, too?"

"They think I have forced you into this."

"She thinks that?"

"Yes. She pleaded with me to give the noble Mister Gilson a chance to work out a great future."

Newlands threw his hand over his head, and his breath caught in a gasp.

"Steady, man," Munroe advised, "you're as hysterical as a schoolgirl."

"And she said nothing else?"

"Nothing," whispered Munroe, but he shuddered as he spoke.

"Don't lie to me," Newlands said. "Why, Jimmy, you're trembling all over. I can feel the bunk shake."

"I must get back to bed," Munroe said. "It won't do for the boys to see me talking with you now."

"But what has happened to upset you, Jimmy?"

"Hell itself has happened, Newlands."

"Hush, you fool, not that name here."

"I'm past thinking of names."

"Bah, you've seen a ghost out of your rotten past, Jimmy."

"A ghost, out of my past, yes. And, my God, what a ghost!"

"Are you backing down on the plan?"

"Not for heaven or hell," Munroe answered hotly with a touch of vibrancy in his whisper. "Tomorrow morning is the time."

"So soon?"

"I tell you, man, we can't wait. They have found me out. They will try to get you to lock me up tomorrow."

"I think they were after that tonight."

"Tonight? Did the old man send for you?"

"Yes. Donnelly spoke to me after he spoke to you. Crawford wanted to see me."

"And you said?"

"The only thing I could say. That I was tired out and having a hard time with the men. That I couldn't come up till tomorrow."

"Did Donnelly insist?"

"He simply looked at me with a queer cast in his eyes as if to say I told you so."

"Damn the fool!"

"He's apt to be that tomorrow. We'll make the break in the morning."

"Yes, you go up to Crawford and tell him that you've come to talk things over. Talk about anything. Tell him you simply can't hold the men."

"And in the meantime you will talk to the men?"

"I'll get them in the new drift, the whole gang, and make a speech to them. A voice carries fine in that place. I'll set them crazy. It will take a regiment of soldiers to keep them in the mine when I get through with them. I'll march them down to Crackens in a mob."

"Good."

"You don't say it as if you mean it. Shake hands on it."

Their hands joined.

"Your hand is like a piece of ice, Billy. Are you weakening in this plan?"

"No, no," came the voice, half whisper and half groan. "I'll do my part. Get away now. I can't stand talking with you any more tonight."

"Bah," answered Munroe, as he rose, "you're like a whipped boy!"

Chapter Twenty-One

GEORGESON'S IDOL TOTTERS

The phrase stayed with Newlands all of a sleepless night. It stuck in his mind when he sat at the breakfast table the next morning. All through the room there was an ominous silence, save in two places.

In one, Georgeson talked with Donnelly. They were the last of the faithful, and he, Gilson himself, was lost to that little number. He stared at his plate and could not eat, for in his ear came the faraway murmur of the other speaking voice. It was Munroe already pouring forth his string of anecdotes and greeted with applause on all sides. He was the indubitable leader now. He had appealed to them on the side where they loved to be stirred.

After breakfast Gilson went to Donnelly and Georgeson and told them that he would not be in the mine that day. Georgeson received the news in silence. Donnelly shrugged his shoulders and scowled at him.

"There's trouble coming up for all three of us," he said. "I suppose you know that, Jim?"

"The men are getting restless," Newlands answered, "but they'll get over it. Put them into the new drift this morning. Crawford wants that run as fast as possible now. I've got to go up to talk with him." He turned and walked back to the bunkhouse.

He was bitterly weary from his sleepless night before, and he lay down on his bunk, but the very posture of repose irritated him. He sat up somewhat dizzily on the edge of the bed. The presence of the crowd of miners still made an atmosphere through the room, although the place was emptied of them.

Newlands took in each detail, almost unconsciously, and then rose and commenced to pace the floor. He had been a power over all these men. He had been something upon which they had to reckon and accord respect. Now he was passing out of their lives. He had abdicated his power as completely as if he had signed a paper. And to whom had he abdicated? He stopped in the midst of his pacing as his imagination called up the picture of Munroe's sallow face. This was his successor.

Before this moment he had never attached any particular glory to his work. He had seen only the fact that he was giving up himself and his labor for the happiness of another man. He had frowned over that thought. Now he found that the pain of the sacrifice had been bittersweet. For he had been able to mold these rough men to his will, use them and push them here and there at his pleasure. But before this very day was over they would stamp him back into this room, and, if they saw him at all, they would give him bare silence—or curses—or, perhaps, they would attempt worse than that. Newlands ground his nails into the palms of his hands and continued his pacing.

After all, the price was richly worth the game. He could go to Beatrice after the mine was closed and disclose himself. She would never dream the part he had played. When she had to choose between him, the man who had attempted to give everything to her happiness, and a man who was an utter failure like Crawford, there could be no doubt of her answer.

She would fall into his arms. That much was surely certain. And yet—he had noted strange things in her before. What if this very failure of Crawford's should be the thing that would make her love him? What if she were a woman who could never truly love until she could give largely?

The thought had never occurred to him when he was listening to the specious talk of Munroe, but now it blanched his face. Yes, yes, that was a possibility. When Crawford was broken and laughed at, she might constitute herself the nurse of his ill fortune as she had been the nurse of his ill health. Perhaps it was her province to give blindly and love where she could give the more completely.

Plodding, heavy steps up the plank walk to the door of the bunkhouse interrupted his thoughts. Donnelly and Georgeson entered the room.

He was standing at the far end of the long room and somewhat in the shadow, and, therefore, he was able to observe them unnoticed for a few moments.

They had been badly battered. The clothes were nearly torn from their bodies in some places, both were bareheaded, Georgeson's face was heavily bruised on one side, and Donnelly held a bandanna handkerchief to his bleeding face as he walked.

They said nothing as they entered. Donnelly went to a pail of water and deliberately began to wash his face. Georgeson dropped upon a bunk and buried his face in his hands. It was he who spoke first.

"It ain't us who matter so much," he said, "but what about th' boss, Jack? What about Gilson that's been keepin' the gang running all this time? What'll he have to say when he hears that we've cleared out?"

Newlands's heart stopped in him as he listened.

Donnelly raised his face slowly from the bucket of water.

Down it ran the little stream of bloody water into the pail with a faint dripping.

"What'll he say?" he repeated heavily. "Damn him, what do I care what he says? Like as not, he's in on the thing. How did Gurney ever get into the mine, except through Gilson?"

Georgeson raised his head and stared at Donnelly in sheer astonishment.

"Easy there, Jack," he said, "that's a good deal of a mouthful for any man to say about Jim Gilson."

"I wish to God he were here to find me saying it," Donnelly hissed. "Little good he did at the mine or to Steve Crawford. The men might as well have walked out three weeks ago as today. That's what I say. I wish he were here to listen to me talkin' now."

"He is," Newlands said quietly, stepping out of the shadow at the end of the room. "He has heard you talk, Jack."

Both men started up to greet him as if he had been an apparition. Donnelly's face hardened.

"If I'm wrong, I'm man enough to admit it," he said after a moment, "but it looks damned queer to me, Gilson."

"What has happened?" Newlands asked, striving desperately to think consecutively. "Have the men turned on you, boys?"

Georgeson was still too confused to answer. He merely looked stupidly to Donnelly.

"Can you look at us and then ask that?" said the latter.

"How did it happen?" was Newlands next question.

"Gurney," answered Donnelly.

"Gurney?"

"Yes, damn him! It's all up with the old Victory Mine, an' all for one no-account man you brought in here, Gilson."

"How could one man raise the crowd?" Newlands asked.

"How could one man stop them when they were about to

raise hell once before, Gilson?" Donnelly questioned bitterly. "You know what a gang is when they get started. You know what one man can do with the mob of them if he ever gets them started. Gurney has them started. Not even you could stop them now. Gilson, tell me, man to man, have you had any part in this here thing?"

Newlands tried to scowl at Donnelly and failed miserably. "I . . . I know nothing," he wavered. "Of course, I know nothing."

"Gurney was your man," continued Donnelly implacably.

"Yes, but how could I tell? How could I know?"

"You were told. Didn't you go to him and talk to him about it, Georgeson?"

Georgeson nodded his head in dumb misery. It was as if he watched an idol fall as he fixed his eye on Newlands. "And why didn't you go down to the mine this morning, if you didn't know something was going to happen?"

"Donnelly," growled Newlands, "if you were a younger and a bigger man, you wouldn't dare to talk like that."

Donnelly stretched an accusing arm toward him. "You haven't answered me yet, Gilson!" he yelled. "You can't answer me."

"Donnelly," Newlands said miserably, "I tell you there is nothing for me to answer."

"You lie," said Donnelly. "Oh, look black if you will. You couldn't choke anything else out of me now. I know you, Gilson. You've been a tool for that dog, Gurney. You ought to be down listening to him, right now."

"He's talking to the men?" Newlands asked faintly.

"He is," Donnelly replied. "We'd no sooner put them to work in the new drift than Gurney gets up and begins to talk, and all the men gather around with their lanterns in their hats and shining in the face of this dog while he talks and tells them that they're fools to work for a fool, and that he's going to leave the mine today. Says he's going to get up and walk out of this place like a man and a free citizen who has some rights in a free country. At that they all start hollerin'. Georgeson and me, we went in among 'em, though we knew it wasn't any use. Even you couldn't have stopped them if you had wanted to. We tried to talk to them, and then they turned on us. You see what happened.

"We didn't have no chance. I tell you they split on us like rain off a shingle. Somebody downed Georgeson. Then they ran both of us out of the drift. Sanderson brought us up in the cage. He didn't say nothing. He just grinned. I tell you he knew what was coming off. So did all of them. Gurney had passed the word. So here's where the old Victory ends. Gurney will be marching the men out of the mine any minute."

"They're still there?" Newlands asked very softly.

"They are."

"Boys," he went on, "will you back me once more?"

"Do what?" cried Donnelly.

"Will you go back to the mine with me?"

"And why?"

"To keep the boys there."

Donnelly laughed unpleasantly. "Don't try that sort of funny stuff on me, Gilson," he said. "I don't like it. They did this to us when they were just starting. Gurney has them like a gang of wolves by this time. They'd eat us alive."

Newlands tore off his jumper with a little ripping sound of the buttons, cast his cap on the floor, and started for the door.

"You're not going?" Georgeson cried. "Man, this is suicide."

"You're mad," Donnelly seconded. "I tell you they're like a pack of wolves. You can't do any good. You could have stopped them an hour ago, maybe. You haven't got a chance now. But, Gilson, thank God I'm wrong. I thought a minute ago that you were hand in glove with Gurney, and it made me sick inside."

Three sharp blasts came from the whistle of the hoisting engine.

"It's too late!" Donnelly moaned. "Don't you see that must be some sort of signal for them to leave the mine?"

Newlands tossed his clenched hands into the air and groaned. "I've got to go," he said. "I can't stay here . . . and wait. Boys, I don't ask you to follow me."

He rushed out of the door, and Georgeson rose as if to follow him.

"Are you going to be a damned fool, too, Georgeson?" Donnelly asked excitedly. "Don't you know that Gilson is going to sure death down there in the drift as soon as the boys spot him?"

Georgeson dropped back upon a bunk and covered his face again, and the two men waited.

But the sound of those three blasts went far and wide over the mountains and rang shrilly in the ears of Crawford and Beatrice. She had wheeled him in his chair outside the cabin door, and from where they were, they could hear the mutter and rumble of the machinery. But after the sound of the blasts, the noise stopped at once and the air was still about them.

They turned startled eyes on one another.

"Donnelly was right," Beatrice said softly.

"No, no," Crawford insisted. "If I can't trust Gilson, whom can I trust? I tell you there is only some accident."

Beatrice smiled faintly. "It is an accident that Gilson has planned," she said. "I am going down to the mine, Steven."

"Beatrice, you shall not," he ordered, straining in his chair. "What if the men should be rising against Gilson?"

She was already halfway down the hill.

193

Chapter Twenty-Two

THE RIGHT TO LAUGH

Newlands stumbled blindly down the entrance to the mine, and then stopped abruptly. A roar of cheering guided him, and he turned and ran swiftly in the dim light down toward the new drift.

The space was quite large and high where he found the miners gathered. They had no tools with them, having dropped them at their places of work to gather around Munroe.

The latter was evidently just concluding his speech. The words came faintly to Newlands.

"And do we go, boys?"

"We do!" came an answering roar that shook the rock walls of the drift.

Newlands could see them gather closer together in the tunnel.

"Are we going to walk out like men?"

"We are!"

"Is there anything this side of hell can stop us?"

A vague roar, into which there went a blending of laughter, answered.

"You at the head, Gurney!" called one great voice.

Again there was the shout of approval.

"You're the general," called another.

There was a commotion among the lights, and Munroe

came to the end of the crowd. They were packing in close behind him as he strode down the drift, whistling over the rush of voices that crammed a thousand echoes against Newlands's ears.

Newlands took up an old pick handle and waited.

Munroe stopped at the head of his column. He could make out a huge, vague figure leaning against the wall of the drift. "Georgeson, you fool, have you come back?" he called.

Newlands threw back his head and laughed. It was a strange sound, and, when it died away in a long series of echoes, there was a cold silence for a moment.

Munroe came closer. "Who's there?" he shouted again, and he leaned over to peer. The remainder of the crowd was several paces behind him. He started as he recognized Newlands. "You utter fool!" he whispered fiercely, close to Newlands. "Turn and run for it. They'll kill you, if they see you now. They still think that you're for Crawford. I didn't dare to tell them you were working with me."

Newlands reached out one long arm and thrust Munroe aside. He went reeling back and struck against the first of the crowd.

"Go back!" thundered Newlands. "Go back, you pack of yellow-hearted curs!"

"Gilson!" called a voice. "It's the big boss!"

"Kill him!" answered another. "He's hounded us enough!"

Munroe came close again. "Have you lost your mind entirely?" he said softly. "There may still be time. I'll try to hold them back. Cut and run now."

"I don't know you!" Newlands roared.

"Billy," Munroe whispered fiercely, "have you double-crossed me? By God, if you have, I'll put this thing through over your dead body, even if I never get a cent!"

"Back!" Newlands growled again. "The first man who comes in reach is dead. Do you hear?"

Munroe shrank back into the crowd.

"Rush him! Rush him!" yelled voices down the tunnel. "Is there any one man can stop us?"

The crowd surged at him with a yell. The drift was large enough to give free play to one man only, and, as the miners plunged toward him, they were packed helplessly shoulder to shoulder in their eagerness.

Into this mass Newlands struck with his club relentlessly as a butcher. The first group fell sprawling in a heap upon the floor of the drift, but the men behind passed over them, yelling and cursing.

Newlands gave back a little farther, pressed by sheer numbers and, as he gave ground, smote again and again into the crowd. For every blow a curse and a yell answered him. It was hot and desperate work. Once they were on him now, he knew that he was worse than dead.

"Kill him!" screamed Munroe's voice over the tumult. "Shall one man stop us? Men, go after him! Let me at him!"

The crowd sprang again at Newlands. They were cunning and hardened fighters in the crowd, and they began to keep back and come at Newlands in smaller fronts, so that each man had play for his arms and body. It was harder work now.

Once the club was half wrenched from Newlands's hands, but he snatched it back again and, seizing it with both hands, jammed it against the nearest faces. They gave back, yelling, then pushed in closer. He swung the pick handle like a quarterstaff. The crowd wavered before him. For he laughed now as he fought and, with the dim light from their lanterns playing in his face, he seemed more devil than man. He leaped among them and struck with the handle, and laughed so that their blood went cold with the sound. It seemed a simple thing to press this madman down by sheer weight of numbers, and after they had him in their hands. . . . They ground their teeth at the thought.

But it was not easy to batter Newlands, whether armed or bare-handed. The pick handle played like a feather in his hands, and it fell with crushing force and lightning rapidity. They forced him back, to be sure, but only step by step. They could never win out of the mine at such a rate of progress.

Munroe worked his way to the front of the mob, and in his hands Newlands saw an ominous glitter.

"Damn you," he screamed, "I'm armed! See if you can fight powder and lead!"

A flash and report followed, and something hummed at Newlands's ear. Before Munroe could fire again, Newlands leaped, ground the revolver from his hand, and tossed it to the floor. Then he raised Munroe bodily above his head and hurled him as if he had been a child into the writhing crowd.

It checked the miners for the moment. Then they saw that Newlands was now unarmed, and the sight heartened them. But with or without weapons he was still far from being beaten.

The fight had now worked back into the narrowest throat of the drift, and the men could come at him only one or two at a time. As they came, he struck savagely and surely, and, where he struck, men fell.

Those weeks of hard labor stood him in stead then. The days of sledge swinging, the days of labor at the pick and shovel, had hardened him wonderfully and given him a machine-like endurance. He fought with the skill of a prize fighter and the strength and calm of a fiend.

The wine of battle was in him. Instead of giving way even a pace before them, he rushed into their front, time and again, and struck with lightning rapidity. Sometimes he crouched and uppercut alternately with those hardened fists. Again he lunged straight forward with heavy drives that struck against the body and broke bones when they landed squarely.

The miners were reaching him with heavy blows in return, and on his shoulders, breast, and face he felt many a stunning impact. It merely maddened him the more, and he leaped at them the more savagely. But somewhere back in his brain he knew that the end was coming. He could feel his strength diminish under the merciless strain. He knew this monstrous battering would leave him weak. He knew, moreover, that at any time might come the emotional reaction and leave him as helpless as a child. He hardly cared. He even gloried in the thought that he should die this way at the hands of rough men, himself mated against all these scores.

Into his thought struck a sound. One other voice he had always been able to recognize above the tumult. It had the high pitch of Munroe. But this voice was lighter, fainter, shriller than Munroe's. It came to him again. It seemed almost as if the sound came from behind him. He drove back into the crowd, and then leaped clear himself. Now, the voice sounded unmistakably clear.

"Jim Gilson! Jim Gilson! Come back! Run! Run! You can escape them yet!"

It was Beatrice. He felt sick at the sound of that voice—and maddened. He sprang into the crowd and beat them back for another breathing space.

"Go back while I hold them!" he shrieked without turning his head. "You fool! There is worse than death, if they take you here!"

He closed on the crowd again. He had hoped that they had not marked the girl, but the glimmer of their lamps down the drift touched on her white dress and a murmur rose into a roar.

"The girl! The girl! Crawford's wife!"

The foul comments that followed that made Newlands

grind his teeth. Unfortunate were those who faced him in that furious moment.

But the end was very near now. He felt himself weakening and turned his head for a fleeting second. His eye fell on Beatrice. She stood tall and white in the shadows. She had not moved since she first called. A deathly sickness came over Newlands. A few moments more and the crowd would be over his body, tearing him to pieces, and after that they would find Beatrice, and then. . . .

The thought gave him strength for a few moments more, but every blow was falling more and more feebly, and now the miners were pressing him back and yelling as they came.

Newlands gave back pace by pace. As he strode, his foot struck on something metallic, and there was a glitter on the floor. Newlands looked down and saw Munroe's revolver. It had lain on the floor unheeded from the moment it dropped from Munroe's hand. He leaned and picked it up.

Into the faces of the nearest he dashed the heavy heel of the weapon, and then, as the crowd checked in its forward surge, again he sprang back for distance and leveled the gun. The crowd halted and shrank. It seemed to every one of them that the leveled gun pointed directly in his face.

"Now, you swine," Newlands gasped, "if you would come to the slaughter, come and be welcome. Here are the lives of five good men in my hand. Who's first?"

There was a growl and further shrinking of the mob.

"Go!" cried Munroe. "He'll misfire, and we'll get him. He'll miss you."

"You talk a hell of a lot too much, Gurney."

"Right!" assented a score of voices. "Shut up, Gurney!"

"Are you going to keep me waiting?" Gilson mocked. "What? Are you going to pick straws to see who goes to sleep first? It's a long time to sleep, boys, but I reckon all of you fellows are tired of life."

A dead silence followed. In his hand there was an argument that admitted of no answer, and not a man of the crowd had the instinct for martyrdom.

"What's the matter?" taunted Newlands. "Have your stomachs turned, my fine wolves? What? You've had the taste of blood this morning, does it make you sick? What?"

There were a few muffled curses, but no direct answer.

"Now, hear me," Newlands called, "you men have listened to a lying dog . . . you have listened to Gurney . . . that's why you are doing this now, isn't it?"

"It is," said one who had been backward in the fighting from the first.

"Gurney is a cur," Newlands declared.

"Damn you," Munroe responded, "you lying hound! Boys, that man had promised to play into our hands, and now he's double-crossing us!"

Newlands laughed again, and, as before, silence followed his laughter.

"Is that the sort of lies you've been feeding the boys on, Gurney?" he called. "What a yellow-hearted cur you are!"

"You'll pay for this in stripes!" Munroe cried.

"Shut up!" shouted one of the men. "Let the boss talk. We've heard enough of you!"

"Right!" shouted a score of voices, for the crowd began to feel that they were doomed to have the worst of the argument and they were glad to find a butt for their anger.

"Boys," called Newlands, "I've worked you hard, but I've played you square! Have I or have I not?"

There was a rumble of agreement.

"Have I met you face to face or have I played behind your backs? Boys, I don't want you to answer that. You know the answer, all of you. But I'll tell you this . . . if Crawford were my worst enemy on God's earth, if he were the man I hated the most and envied the most, I would fight you to a death for something more than his sake. Can you dream what that is?"

They stared at him blankly, but Beatrice, far back among the shadows of the drift, started and crouched closer against the wall of the drift, as if in fear.

It was a real fear, for as she listened to that voice, hoarsened now with mighty labor, it brought back to her the thought of another voice that she had known long before. She turned and fled farther down the drift.

"I tell you," went on Newlands, "I'm going to play square in this game, and I'm going to make you play square, if I have to murder you to do it. Understand? Now, I'm going to make an offer of compromise. You're sick of the mine. Well, listen to this. You still have ten days to work in the mine on contract. What do you say if Crawford meets you halfway and cuts the time down to five days with three dollars a day more pay? Does that sound good to you?"

"Where's your authority?" Munroe shouted. "Show your authority for that offer."

"You keep still or I'll choke you with mud," spoke up a voice that Newlands knew to be one of the Upton brothers.

"I've lived up to every other promise," Newlands stated. "Do you think I'll keep this?"

"You're all right," said someone. "We'll take him, boys, eh? It's only for a few days!"

Newlands knew that he dared not press the point then. The crowd was obviously with him, but they were a bruised and angered lot. "All right," he said. "I take your word for it as you take mine. No more work this morning. We'll start again at noon. If anyone is hurt, he can go up to Crawford's house and get fixed up. Boys, I'm willing to trust to you." He made good his remark by tossing his revolver on the ground.

The first few men made a start toward him by instinct, but checked themselves instantly.

Miners, on the whole, love fair play, and this crowd was remembering that Newlands had always been a man to them, was above all a man now and accepting them as such. There was an instant of pause, and then a hoarse cheer that shook the drift and brought down a little shower of gravel and dirt.

Newlands turned on his heel and strode back toward the entrance of the mine. The great sense of weakness and loss came on him now. He had won, indeed, but at what a cost. He had won for another man and given to another man something dearer than life to him. He leaned for a moment against the wall of the drift and passed a hand across his battered and bleeding forehead, and then went on. Into his mind as he walked, stumbling over every uneven bit of ground, there passed a hundred thoughts at once.

He knew well enough that Munroe would be maddened into the last resort of action now. He would slip away from the mine and go to Crackens with the information that would make Newlands a refugee from the law. Perhaps he could induce Crawford easily enough to hold Munroe by force at the mine. But that would only be delaying the inevitable.

The day was near when a man would touch him on the shoulder and say: "William Newlands, I arrest you in the name of the law."

Yet all this he could have avoided if he had played the game as Munroe outlined it to him. The cards were dealt. Everything as Munroe had said was falling into his hand. Everything, perhaps, except love. But at the least he would have had Beatrice. Newlands threw back his head and laughed again, a great mirthless laugh that rang through the tunnel and broke off short. For he saw a few paces away a glitter of faint light on a white dress and knew that Beatrice was standing before him.

"I have seen," she said faintly. She came to him and caught his broken hands in her cool ones. "I never dreamed that God could make such a man," she whispered. "Never dreamed that there could have been such a man as you." She paused a moment and gave a choking little laugh. "And all the while," she breathed, "I thought . . . I thought . . . ah, God, what a fool I have been."

She became aware that he had made no answer and stood staring stupidly at her.

"You are hurt," she said. "You are badly hurt. Come, lean on me. See, I am very strong."

She passed her arm around his body and drew one large arm over her shoulder. They stood so a moment. His shirt, tattered and wet with sweat, pressed against her cheek. His whole body trembled with utter exhaustion. And she heard his breath drawn in long gasps.

"You must come," she said. "Don't talk if you wish not to. Come. See, I can help you." She was talking to him as to a child who could not quite understand her words.

He stopped and removed her arm, pushing her away from him. Then he reeled a pace back and threw out his arms until he stood looming like a cross against the wall of the drift.

"Go back!" he commanded. "Go back to the nursery from which you came. Go back to your sick man. How can such a man as I have a need of you? Go back to Crawford, for he has won this day, won success, and fortune and fame to put at your feet. And I? What have I won? The right to laugh!"

He turned away from her, and she could see the big outline of his figure stumbling and wavering through the shadows, and ever the strangely shrill mockery of his laughter rang back to her.

Chapter Twenty-Three

THE WEALTH OF SOLOMON

Beatrice saw Newlands stop at the mouth of the tunnel, looming black against the white day, and she hurried after him with steps that stumbled over the uneven footing. She hardly knew why, but she felt that she must be with him, that there was some need he had of her. Yet, when she came closer to him, her emotions were lost in a blending of fear and awe, for he stood now, erect and facing into the wind that blew down the tunnel mouth. Already the weariness seemed to have dropped from his poised body, and he was ready for renewed battlings.

Half of his shirt had been ripped away, so that it depended now from one shoulder, and the other arm showed alive with flexing muscles and glittering in the light. As he turned at her step, she saw a face streaked with blood down one side, black with a beard of many days' growth, and above it the thick hair, rumpled and astir with the wind.

The words that had formed in her mind stopped on her lips at that sight. He had seemed to her the moment before a broken and wounded man, scarcely able to support his own weight. He looked now a berserker prepared for battle. Still she stepped toward him. Her hand moved out in a gesture that might have been appeal and might have been question. But he met her eye coldly and waved her away from him and out of the tunnel.

She would have stopped, even then. She would have proffered him some assistance and care, but to proffer assistance to this man seemed like offering sympathy to a mountain because a storm has bruised its front. She watched him turn and swing back into the gloom of the tunnel, and she stepped out into the daylight.

As she walked up the hill, her eyes went up by instinct to those peaks which stood up with sentinel white heads against the pallor of the upper sky, and, as she stepped up the mountainside, she found herself walking with a longer and more buoyant stride. Then her eyes averted suddenly to the cabin up the hill, and the solitary figure in the chair seated before it. She stood a moment at gaze, and then turned, on an impulse, and shifted her course up the valley.

It seemed to her in that instant that all her life at the Victory Mine had been cramped and meaningless, and all her work for Crawford worthless, not to be weighed with real endeavor. It was a bitter moment for her, and, as she walked, she felt that a dream fell shattered about her at every step. It was as if she were walking into a reality of life up this valley, where she had walked a hundred times before, and found nothing.

She did not know how long she walked, or when she turned back, but at last she found herself again near the cabin, and she turned toward it with a sigh. Georgeson passed her as she went up the hill.

He had evidently made some report, for when she came toward Crawford, he called gaily, while she was still a long way off: "Hurry up! I want a real description of what happened." And when she came close: "Were you really there? Did you see the fight?"

"All of it."

"By Jove! Let's hear, then! These fellows have no tongues to talk. Besides, Georgeson only has it as second-hand. Give me the real thing."

She paused a moment, casting about in her mind for words, and, as the picture came back stronger and brighter in her thought, she straightened, her nostrils widened, her lips curved into a stern smile, half fierce and half happy.

But it happened that the wind, which had been blowing steadily and softly, quickened to a sudden angry gust, and whistled and sang sharply among the pines about the cabin. Beatrice looked down wonderingly into Crawford's face.

He was unchanged, smilingly expectant. He was unchanged, but a whole world had broken and toppled about her in this last hour.

She cast her arms out in a little gesture of abandon. "I cannot talk," she said rapidly. "I have to think it out to myself before I can talk it to anyone else."

And so she left him and went into the house. A little later he heard her singing "The Slave," her voice filling wonderfully on the last notes:

> My name is Mahomet. I am from Yemen,
> And my line is that of Asra,
> Who die when they love.

Then, very plaintively, the soft repetition:

> Who die when they love!

Crawford swerved in his chair and listened tensely. It was all very strange to him. He would have called her, but Donnelly was coming up the hill with another report, and his mind was flooded with business the next moment.

Donnelly was still bearing the marks of the conflict of earlier morning, but his face was bright. "They're back at it again!" he shouted in greeting.

"But it isn't noon!" exclaimed Crawford. "I thought Gilson had given them the rest of the morning off."

"He did." Donnelly grinned, panting from his hasty walk up the hillside. "But they didn't want any lay-off. They pitched in, an', now they're tearin' the heart out o' the mountain. Ah, it's a sight to warm your heart, Steve!"

"An hour ago they were for marching out, now they won't even take a lay-off," pondered Crawford heavily. "How do you make it out, Jack?"

"I don't know," Donnelly admitted. "I don't give a damn why it is. All I know is that it's so. An' you should see them work!"

"Has Gurney gone back to work with them?"

Donnelly threw back his head and laughed hoarsely. "Him? Not a hope," he stated. "He started to, well enough, but he didn't get far. The boys began to rough-house him. They hold it against him because he pulled a gun on Gilson in the fight. And them all tryin' to get at Gilson themselves. Now all they remember is that Gurney tried some dirty work."

"Did they beat him up badly?" Crawford queried, with an expression that was not untouched with pleasure.

"They would have," said Donnelly, "but Gilson stepped in again and stopped them. Old Sanderson was about to swing a pick handle on Gurney's head when Gilson up and grabbed his arm and backed Gurney out of the mob. They lay all of the uprising on Gurney now, and they're pretty sore at him. They made Gilson promise to keep him close before they'd let Gurney go. So he sent me and Georgeson down to the shanty outside the bunkhouse to tie up Gurney and leave him there, with Georgeson standing guard. I twisted a chain around his ankles and left him there, with a box to sit on and a newspaper to amuse him. He sure ain't going to get away in a hurry. But he's a cool one, all right. Never a word all the time, just quiet and smilin', but there's all hell in his heart. Gilson came down with us to watch us tie him, and Gurney looked at him all the time. I got an idea life will get exciting for Gilson when Gurney gets loose again."

"He'll never get loose, Jack," Crawford said grimly. "There are ways of putting the law on a man of his type, and, by God, I'll see that it's done!"

"Right," agreed Donnelly. "He needs the law. One man would have to have eyes in the back of his head to watch him. Steve, I've got so damned interested talkin' about Gurney I've forgot to tell you they're uncoverin' another bit of good ore down there."

Crawford shook his head and sat back in his chair with a rather weary smile. "Donnelly," he said, "I'm not thrilled. It's the same old scare over again. I know. It's merely a smell of the real thing. Now that the game is so nearly done, Jack, I don't mind telling you that I'm through hoping. We had a chance with ten days ahead of us. With only five days left, our chances go down to about zero."

Donnelly scratched his chin and looked sidewise, and then drew a deep breath. "I thought it might cheer you up," he said, grinning rather sheepishly, "but I got an idea you're right, Steve."

He talked for another moment uneasily, and then went on back to the mine.

Crawford sat quietly and turned his eyes from the valley to the mountains and back again to the valley.

The warmth of the sun and the chill of the breeze played on him till there was no bitterness in his thoughts as he pondered his failure, but merely a dim sense of expectancy. He was almost glad that the time that was left before he would be an acknowledged failure was short and the strain of the long wait would be over.

The rattling of the pans in the kitchen and the singing of Beatrice came to him clearly in little bursts of sound, and he listened and wondered. He had never fully understood her. She seemed miles away from him now, and there was infinite hurt in the thought.

The sad drifting of the wind through the winnowed pine needles roused him again from his dreaming. He drew the watch from his pocket and glanced at it, started, and glanced again. It was well past the noon hour, and yet he had seen none of the miners come out of the mine. He held his watch close against his ear to make sure that it was running. Then he frowned down at the mine again. It was truly a day of mystery.

Almost at the same instant a black speck appeared at the entrance to the mine. At last, he thought, the men were coming out for the noon hour. But this speck resolved itself into a single man who ran up the hillside toward him.

Crawford leaned back in his chair and watched closely. From the size of the man it must be either Georgeson or Gilson. If it were Gilson, there was trouble again in the mine. If it were Georgeson. . . .

Crawford covered his face with one hand and waited. When he looked again, Georgeson was close upon him and panting as he ran. He stopped a moment to wave his crumpled hat. "We've got it!" he yelled. "We've knocked the cap off a bed of ore that'll make you richer'n Solomon, Mister Crawford!"

Crawford stiffened in his chair.

"The boys are all crazy," continued Georgeson, as he

came closer to the chair. "They've heard the news, and they won't stop. They won't even stop to eat. The old fever has got them all going south. Mister Crawford, I'm here to congratulate you. There ain't nobody in these here mountains but will be doin' the same thing before long."

Crawford took the big hand weakly and stared straight into Georgeson's eyes. He said slowly: "You're a pretty young chap, but you're an old miner. Are you sure about this?"

"Mister Crawford," he answered, "I only wish you were down there to see her open up."

"What does Donnelly think?"

Georgeson broke into a laugh that was like the roar of a bull. "He stopped thinkin', along with everybody else in the mine, except Gilson. Donnelly's ravin' and tearin' around like a two-year-old colt. You'd think he was drunk, to hear him talk. To tell you straight, I wasn't much better myself. Gilson made me come up here to tell you, or I'd be down there yellin' my head off now, with the rest of them. Listen!"

Faint and shrill through the air came the sound of many voices from the gaping entrance to the mine.

"That's the way down there," went on Georgeson. "They work like the devil for half an hour, and then all at once someone starts cheerin', and then back at work again."

Crawford sat back in his chair, white and weak. Still he could not convince himself that he had really heard truly. "Gilson," he said faintly, "why didn't he come to tell me?"

"You'll have to ask him," Georgeson said joyously. "I don't know. He keeps drivin' them on and says he won't leave till he's sure it's no false alarm. I'm goin' back. I wouldn't miss this for a year of livin'."

He whirled and started rapidly down the mountainside again.

Chapter Twenty-Four

JIM GILSON SAYS GOOD BYE

"Beatrice!" called Crawford.

She came, with her sleeves rolled up to the elbows, and a dish towel over one arm.

"Did you hear?"

"No."

"Then come here and sit down. I want to tell you slowly. It's almost more than one can understand."

She came obediently and sat on the arm of the chair. She was half smiling, and her eyes were strangely distant, but she sobered at the sight of his tremulous excitement.

"I don't know how to put it," Crawford began. "I feel almost religious, as if there were something stronger than human will in my life for the last two months. It seems as if there had been fate behind all this. You came to me when no one else could have saved my life, and then Gilson came when the work of that life was about to fail, and now, today. . . . Beatrice. . . ."

She sprang up from the chair with a glad little shout. "Gold! Gold! Gold!" she cried. "Oh, Steve, dear, I knew! I knew!"

He stared at her somewhat wildly. "You knew?"

"Of course," she said. "Do you think that such a man's work could go for nothing? He had to win, had to win!" She leaned over him and framed his face suddenly with her hands. "Because failure isn't the destiny of such a man, Steve," she concluded.

He caught one of her hands. "And you see what it means to me . . . to us?" he asked eagerly. "A home . . . riches . . . servants . . . everything that can make life livable, Beatrice?"

"But just now," she cried, breaking away from him, "it means burned biscuits unless I get back into the kitchen!"

She fled into the house, and a moment later her singing floated out to him. But Crawford turned his head and frowned as he listened. He would have given a great deal to have been with her when she saw the fight in the mine that morning.

The swift events of the afternoon strode one after the other upon his attention. The reports came every few minutes. Each was more convincing than the last.

By two o'clock everyone in the mine was sure of the big strike. By three o'clock even the pessimism of Crawford began to give way to smiles. By four o'clock he was finally convinced.

He sent for Donnelly and gave him a long telegram that had to be sent to the investment company from Crackens. He ordered Newlands to stop the work of the men and tell them they were at liberty to go where they pleased, and that the train was at their service to take them to Crackens to celebrate.

As he sat back in his chair and watched the black, crowding specks that were men swarming from the mine hurriedly, and afterward heard the rapid chortling of the engine as it puffed down the valley, it seemed to Crawford that he could describe in himself the emotions of the great general who looks over the stricken field and counts the cost and the glory of his success and is content.

Beatrice wheeled his chair back into the cabin, and he sat waiting for Newlands to appear. He had sent for him twice before, and each time his foreman had put off his appearance with the excuse that there was still work to do.

There could be nothing now, and yet minute after minute passed, and evening was close on them before he saw Gilson, hatless, pacing up the mountainside.

While he was still a long way off, Crawford perceived a change in the approaching man. He walked with a slight crouch of peculiar alertness. His arms swung loosely at his side, with the hands half closed, as if he had just relinquished some tool. His steps were heavy and lunging, as if he were in haste to leave the old work behind him and reach the new. And now, as he came closer, Crawford could mark his face. A fringe of dark hair shadowed the sunken cheeks and the great furrows that slanted past the corners of his mouth. As he came yet nearer, Crawford saw that his muscles were set taut, and the brows heavily converging, as if he were keeping his mind concentrated to some purpose, with an almost physical effort.

It had seemed to Crawford before that Gilson was only maintained in his prodigious efforts in the mine by forgetfulness of all, save one ultimate goal of his labor. But that goal must have been the discovery of the gold, and, if that were the case, it was reached and passed.

Still his face carried the imprint of a driving purpose, and the eyes looked straight forward and passed beyond him. He was not like a man out-wearied, but one nerving himself to the last effort, like a runner who enters the homestretch with a crowd of competitors on his heels.

Crawford felt a strange emotion of suspense. He turned his head toward Beatrice and saw that she, too, had grown somewhat white and lingered nervously. So, at last, when Newlands towered at the entrance to the cabin, all three were silent through a moment.

"Gilson," Crawford said, "you know why I've sent for you?"

It seemed to Crawford that the hint of a smile struggled faintly for a moment with the set lines of the foreman's face.

"I do," he said.

Crawford frowned a little in his surprise. "You know?"

"You are going to offer me money," Newlands said quietly.

Crawford flushed. "Not in pay," he said eagerly. "It is just breaking into my mind that money means nothing to you, Gilson. But I want you to share the profits of this thing with me."

The smile was now apparent on Newlands's face. He waved his hand carelessly in dismissal of the idea.

"The ore will run between thirty-five and forty dollars a ton, at the very least," Crawford stated with marked emphasis.

"I am very glad," said Newlands.

"And I want you to take a percentage of the returns."

Newlands stared at him as if he did not understand.

"I want you to share in the returns," Crawford repeated clumsily. "I want to make some returns where they belong."

"As nearly as I can make out," Newlands said slowly, "this means that you are rich, that your reputation is established."

"I suppose that it does," Crawford responded.

"That," continued Newlands, "is what I was working for. The rest doesn't matter a damn. I don't want your money. I have saved a good lot of my wages. Tonight I start away. I wish you all the luck in the future."

Crawford looked desperately about the room as if in

search of something to make his position stronger. In doing so his eye fell upon Beatrice. She stood by the entrance to the kitchen, one arm braced against the doorjamb and her head drooping.

"Beatrice," he called, "won't you talk to Gilson? Won't you tell him that he's making a fool of himself?"

She raised her head very slowly and met his eyes with a wan smile. "I have nothing to say," she replied.

Crawford turned almost angrily back upon Newlands. "Do you think I don't understand?" he shouted. "Do you think I am blind to the fact that, if it had not been for you, I would never have made a cent out of the old Victory? Don't I remember the day you first came, and how you stopped the miners when they were about to walk out for all of me? Can't I remember how you have kept them at work day after day when no other man on God's green earth could have moved them to budge a single pick or shovel? Man, I'm not blind! I owe all this to you. There is only one way I can pay you back. Mark me here. I don't offer you a set sum. I offer you a share in the profits as one man to another. You can name the share you want. Is that what's holding you back?"

Newlands regarded him for a long moment, and the smile that finally came was almost sad. He stepped to Crawford and took his hand again, but this time with a great grip that made the engineer wince and rub his hand afterward. "I'm glad," Newlands said, "I'm damned glad that you're this kind of a man, Crawford. I had an idea that you were, but there was a time when I wouldn't admit it to myself. Now I know. And I'm gladder than you'll ever dream." He threw back his head and laughed.

Both Beatrice and Crawford started. They had heard that short laugh before.

"There is only one thing left for me to do before I leave the

Victory Mine," went on Newlands, "and it has nothing to do with money from you or the Victory Mine, Crawford. It is to set Gurney loose."

"Set Gurney loose!" broke in Crawford. "Good God, man, you can't do that! I have meant to tell you what Donnelly said to me. He is sure that Gurney has some grudge against you, Gilson. Perhaps it is because you chained him today. Listen to me, Gilson. There are ways in which we can detain him at least until he gets over his malice. Let me try. It's a little thing, Gilson, but it may be to your benefit."

Newlands flung his hand with an ugly gesture, and for a moment his face hardened into what was almost hate. Crawford shrank back a little in his chair, astonished.

"You can't offer me anything, Crawford," he said, after a moment in which his breath was drawn in a hiss. "There's nothing on earth which can repay me. Only the knowledge that I have mined happiness for two people. Such happiness!"

Again he broke into the short laugh. It seemed to Crawford that he heard an echo to it in the back of the room, and he turned his head hastily, but Beatrice was turning toward the kitchen.

"As for Gurney," Newlands continued, "he shall go free. No one shall cross me in this. Then I'm going to ride into the higher mountains. I have a strange desire for travel. There's nothing to do but say good bye. I say it now."

"Wait!" Crawford begged as the larger man turned. "You can't leave me like this, Gilson. Take my hand, anyway, and tell me that someday you'll come back and ask some reward at my hands. Everything I have will be yours."

Newlands hesitated, and then stretched out his hand slowly toward Crawford. But before the fingers crossed, he drew back his arm hastily and, with a sort of shudder, turned away and half ran down the slope.

Chapter Twenty-Five

TWO OLD FRIENDS PART COMPANY

He changed his shambling run into a long, striding walk before he reached the pit of the valley. The long mountain evening had already begun. Over an eastern peak the bronzed moon rose steady through the purple and blue of the sunset sky, lingered a moment among the tops of the distant pines, and then floated up the heavens. For a colorful half hour it would struggle against the more glaring light of the day, and then, growing paler and paler, reign supreme over mountain and valley. A song sparrow twittered furtively in the nearest sugar pine, and Newlands stopped to listen vaguely. As he did so, he thought that he heard another step behind him halt a moment after his.

He whirled and stared behind him. He saw nothing save the straight trunks of the sugar pines. He almost smiled to himself at his fantasy as he turned again and resumed his way toward the bunkhouse.

He lighted a lantern in the bunkhouse, for it was now quite dark, and then went with it to the little adjoining shed where Munroe was confined. Munroe was curled up in a corner fast asleep.

He roused himself and sat up, rubbing his eyes and yawning when Newlands stirred him with his foot. He considered his visitor without surprise, and sat hugging his knees to his chest and staring at him. Newlands stooped and examined the chain that fettered the captive.

"I've only got a small file," he said, "but I guess it will do the work on that wire."

Munroe started to his feet so violently that he collided with the bent figure of Newlands. "Do the work?" he queried.

Newlands examined him with contemptuous wonder. "You thought I would leave you here for the miners to beat up when they get back?"

Munroe peered anxiously into his face, which was somewhat obscured by the shadow of the lantern. "You are really going to set me loose?" he asked.

Newlands shrugged his shoulders.

"Of course," Munroe said slowly, "there's nothing else for your sort of man to do, Newlands." Then, as a new thought occurred to him, he started again and took Newlands by the shoulders. "Billy," he said grimly, "do you really think you are squaring things with me by doing this?"

"Take your hands away," Newlands demanded coldly. "They make my flesh cold clear through the clothes."

Munroe dropped his hands with a whispered curse.

"No," said Newlands. "I expect nothing from you."

"Except everything in my power to put you behind the bars, eh, Billy, my boy?" finished Munroe.

Again Newlands shrugged his shoulders. "You can't do that," he said calmly. "I don't like life that much."

Munroe regarded him almost with admiration. "Right," he said. "There's no bluff in you nowadays, Billy. The mountains have changed you. By the Lord, I think even now I'd forgive you and let the past be past. But you shamed me before a crowd of men, Newlands. You know no one can get away with that with me."

"Of course not," agreed Newlands.

Neither of them raised their voices as they spoke. They understood each other too perfectly.

"You can't hold me up on the Edgerley deal now, Jim," Newlands reminded him. "You know that the G. and W. stock has returned my investment by now. That scare is done."

"That isn't needed. It isn't only the fake marriage or the Edgerley deal I have on you," went on Munroe. "You understand I have enough stuff on you to pen you up for half the rest of your life. They aren't bad things, but strung together they make a bad story, eh?"

Newlands reached out a hand and tilted Munroe's face. It showed very pale but unafraid in the lantern light.

"Singular, Jimmy, isn't it?" he said. "It would be easy enough for me to strangle you here without a sound and then take your body into the gorge up there a ways and leave you to rot. No one would ever know."

"Of course not," agreed Munroe. "They'd think I'd gotten free and gone back to Crackens and from there to God knows where."

"Why can't I do it?" asked Newlands.

"You can't get rid of me that way," Munroe said, still in the conversational tone that they both had adopted. "You haven't got the courage for murder in cold blood. You were always a quitter when it came to the real thing."

Newlands bent over and began to file at the wire that joined the chains around Munroe's ankles. "If I let you loose," he went on in the same dead voice, "you will go down to Crackens and give the sheriff word about me, won't you?"

"Sure," said Munroe amiably, "and then you'll get ready for a long trip through the hills, eh?"

The grating of a file filled in a pause.

"It'll probably be a long chase," he went on, "and before it ends you'll go through all the hells of hunger and thirst and all that, eh, Billy? But in the end we'll get you. Of course, you understand all that?"

Newlands filed through the last wire, untwisted the chains, and rose to his feet.

"Jimmy," he said, "all I want to know is . . . will you come with them, armed, for the sake of running me down? Will you be armed to the teeth, as they say in the books, so that it'll be an even chance between us?"

"Billy," Munroe responded, "I swear I'll carry a gun in each pocket and one in each hand."

Newlands stared at him a moment longer, and then leaned and unlocked the shackles.

Munroe yawned, stretched himself, and yawned again. "This gives you about twelve hours' head start," he said. "But what's twelve hours in the mountains?" He waved a casual arm. "Nothing," he said. "Nothing, my dear boy."

"It'll be hard on you if you meet any of our boys in Crackens," said Newlands. "Are you armed now?"

"A hunting knife," Munroe answered, "and I know how to use it." He tapped his hip pocket as he spoke.

Newlands backed out into the moonlight. Munroe passed him and stepped off down the valley, fading among the shadows of the sugar pines.

After Munroe disappeared, Newlands went back to the main room of the big bunkhouse. It was quite deserted. The single lantern that always illuminated the room had not been filled, and it sent out a weird light, flickering sometimes high and sometimes low, as if it were making a strong effort to keep up its work.

"Singleton has neglected his job," growled Newlands, speaking aloud. "I'll have to bring him up short for it in the morning." He broke off and laughed shortly. In the morning he would be a refugee from the law, hunted like a catamount through the wilderness.

He went over to his bunk and found, by dint of much fumbling, some articles which he needed—a razor, a number of cartridges for the revolver in his hip pocket that he had carried since the uprising, three heavy shirts, two blankets, a pair of boots, because he would need them for riding through the hills, a leather coat that would be invaluable against the sudden mountain downpours. He pulled on the boots and made the articles into a compact bundle that he fastened by means of a stout cord. As he rose from the bunk and turned, he started at the sound of a foot pausing at the door. He frowned.

Perhaps it was Munroe come back to him. It would be hard on Munroe if this were true. There came an unmistakable tapping at the door.

"Come in!" Newlands shouted.

A silence followed.

Newlands drew out his revolver and examined it hastily.

The tapping came again.

"Come in!" called Newlands again, and then, as no move of the door answered him, he commenced tiptoeing lightly toward it. This must certainly be Munroe. What a fool he was to play so old a trick in a time like this.

He flung the door wide and, springing with the same movement back into the shadow, leveled his revolver.

Beatrice stood in the moonlit square.

She did not see him at first. The interior was so much dimmer than the keen moonlight that she could hardly look into the shadows, so she shaded her eyes with one hand and peered closely.

"Billy!" she called in a faint voice. "Billy Newlands!"

Chapter Twenty-Six

"I HAVE BEEN SO BLIND!"

The revolver rattled heavily on the floor, and, at the sound, Beatrice stepped quickly back into the night. A vagrant breath of wind caught at her dress and set it fluttering. It was a white, cheap dress that a kitchen servant would not have envied. But it hung fresh and clean and jaunty, and gave close to the curve of her body.

Newlands stepped to the door and leaned there, braced on either side by a hand gripping the doorjamb. His eyes were heavily on her. He saw that she had gone very pale and with one hand behind her as if she were feeling for support.

"Billy," she said, "Billy, I have been so blind!"

They stood for another long moment waiting for they knew not what, and staring at each other.

His eye went little by little over the slender figure with the white dress fluttering about her, the white figure that seemed to lilt and wave to every stir of the wind. When he came to her eyes, his glance stopped and plunged deep. She in turn studied every line of the grime-streaked, grim face with the brows above. And there was fear and wonder and something else in her heart. She could not name the last.

He made a long step toward her, and she recoiled instinctively. At the recoil she saw his face contract and his eyes narrow. He came to a quick stop.

"You know?" he asked heavily.

"I . . . I have known in my heart all the time," she answered, and the steadiness of her voice surprised her. "And now a bolt has been shot back somewhere in me, and I understand."

He half turned from her again with his head drooped between the big shoulders. Now, truly, she remembered it all. She remembered that he had first stood in that posture when he had told her that he loved her and asked her to marry him. But now how different it was—this soiled, grim-faced giant, in contrast with that other Billy Newlands marked with the sleekness of fat living, flabby with dissipation. Yes, many things that she had not been able to guess, then, were patent to her now.

He did not turn back to face her. He talked half turned away and with his frown directed at the wall. "I have not come to claim you," he said. "I have no right. I have no right!"

"How can you do away with that right by speaking?" she queried. "Isn't it something more than words can break?"

He gestured in dumb disavowal. It seemed as if he had neither heart nor breath to speak.

"What has it all meant?" she went on, praying that he would look at her in that moment. "What has your service to Steven meant, and the coming of Gurney, and his talk with you, and his knowledge of my past? What has the whole grim secret been?"

He pushed a hand through his hair, and still his eyes did not turn. She saw his hand was trembling and a wonder took her that such strength could be tremulous.

"I have come to tell you everything," he answered, "and now I find that it is harder than I knew. I have served Crawford because it means your happiness. Your happiness

is his success. I am not blind. You are meant for each other.
You brought him back from death. He will bring you to honor
and content. So be it."

He stopped a moment, and she saw him shiver.

"Gurney," he began, and stopped again. "Gurney . . .
knew," he went on, pausing between each word he spoke as if
each required a separate thought, "about you . . . and about
me. He knew . . . that we were not man and wife."

She did not move from where she stood, merely parted her
lips to speak perhaps in protest. But Newlands never knew.
He talked on with his eyes steadily before him.

"The marriage was no marriage," he said. "The minister
was Gurney."

She cried out at that. But it was not a cry so much as a
moan, and she checked it at the sight of this man in his agony,
this great bulk of power shaken and unnerved by mere words.

"I had made up my mind before I met you," he went on.
"The whole thing was arranged in my thought. I needed
money. I would have taken yours. I would not have married
you honestly to get it." He raised his head, and his eyes were
wide with vision. "I remember how you came down the gangplank the morning I first met you," he said, "with the big
longshoreman framing you behind. That moment you walked
into my life and my heart. I didn't know it. I never knew I
truly loved you then or in the after days. I knew that you were
good, that you were beautiful, that you were sent to me in
trust . . . and that you could be used."

He locked his hands behind his head, and his big body
quivered. "Then came the day of the wedding," he went on,
driving himself remorselessly in the confession. "That was
the first time I began to suspect that . . . that I might not be
able to go through with it. Do you remember that when you
went to your room after the . . . after the wedding . . . you sang

a song? It sings in my mind still. I had to find courage to go ahead then. I drank."

She shivered slightly, remembering that gruesome wedding breakfast, the dulled eyes of the groom, the hand that had fallen lingeringly upon her arm, the long nightmare on the train that day. And now this.

"I drank," he said, "to find courage. And I found it. And then came the wreck. Then I went into these mountains and I discovered many things . . . about myself . . . that I had never known. So I finally came here."

She raised her head, but she saw that he was still looking away from her. The silence grew desperate to her.

"And when you found me?" she asked at last.

"When I found you," he said, "I saw that there was a way to serve you. I took that way."

"But you have served another man," she contradicted. "You have slaved as a common laborer in a mine, and you have torn a fortune out of the heart of the earth for another man, and you have not taken my money . . . and . . . and why . . . why, why?"

Still for an instant he remained silent and staring at the wall, and then, as if an impulse stronger than him drew him toward her, he turned very slowly and went to her in a few slow steps with a pause between each move as if he would have stopped even then if he could.

When he came back to her, he tilted her face back and stared fiercely into her eyes.

Even then she wondered, not because he had touched her, but because the hand that touched her was as tremulous as that of an excited woman.

"Then I found that I loved you," he said. "I found myself hungering miserably for you, and desperate. And so I served you like a slave because I thought that I could win you happiness . . . and I have." He turned from her suddenly and tossed his hand up in the air.

"Do you think I have not cursed every stroke of work I have done here, knowing that it was done for him? Oh, I have worked myself to madness because I dared not stop to think. I dared not stop to remember or to see. I have waked up suddenly in the night, and it was as if a presence were standing by me and talking with me. The very shadows took shapes. The very silence had a voice. The wind in the trees outside wailed one song to madness. Pah! You cannot understand. You have not a heart to understand. You are cold. You are not worthy of a great desire. Beatrice, go back! Go back to the man on the hill, for I have won happiness for you both."

He broke off, and laughed, and the sound ended in a gasp. "Wasn't it worth the struggle?" he queried hotly. "Wasn't it worth the hell on earth to win for you? I have given you to a fine, clean, strong man . . . damn him forever! I have ripped open a mountain to make him rich and successful . . . curse him! I have given the blood out of my heart, drop by drop. Oh, may he rot in hell . . . he has fame, riches, success . . . and you! God help me."

He leaned suddenly and swept her into arms that tortured her with their pressure. "And all the while I have loved you," he said in a quiet voice that tore her inwardly. "All the while I have been maddened for you. I have drawn your face through the hours of the night. I have fought and sweated through the day to drive those same lines out of my mind again. I have hungered for you . . . to take you in my arms as I take you now . . . to kiss your lips . . . as I kiss them now. My rose of all the world . . . there is a perfume in your breath that strikes all my soul to a drunken riot. I may touch your eyes . . . and the softness of your body is fallen against me . . . and your head falls back . . . your eyes stare into mine . . . shall this not be the last surrender? Is there nothing in bodily possession?"

She felt his whole body tense against her and saw the madness come in his eyes, and she knew that she must meet that stare and meet it without defiance or she was lost. Yet she knew that she was helpless. Two strange pictures drove one another through her mind. There was one of the bloated face that had leered above her berth in the Pullman car and the form that had swayed with the lurching. The other was a picture of the dim-lighted drift, of the giant meeting the cursing throng of miners single-handedly, of the tumult of action, of the conquest of those strong wills by one still stronger. And now this same force grappled her. But the sense of that force sent a mighty singing in her blood.

He shook her away suddenly to arm's length.

"But the soul is beyond my power," he muttered, "and the soul is you. I cannot hold that in my arms."

She placed herself in his arms again. She could not see clearly. She could not think clearly. She only knew that this thing was right.

"Yes, yes," she said fiercely. "You have taken my soul in the hollow of your hand to mold as you will and hold forever. I have come to you to tell you that. There is none of me that is not yours."

He only stared at her blankly.

"You must understand," she insisted with a changed voice. "Look at me! There is nothing in me that does not go out to you . . . does not need you!"

He raised a long arm and pointed dumbly up the hill.

"He?" she queried, and then brushed the thought away with an impatient arm. "He has his work and the success that you have won for him. They will fill his heart. I have told him. I told him that I gave myself to you once in speech, and never knew how completely words might bind the heart. I have left him forever. I have no care if no minister has wedded us. I spoke that day for God to hear and not for any man."

She pushed his arm aside and pressed close to him. "You need me, dearest," she said, "and I you. We can be married again in truth. And you shall take me forever."

He flung her away from him suddenly so that she struck forcibly against the wall.

"It is not the false marriage only," he said slowly. "If I had known this! But I never dreamed. I had no care for life. And so Munroe slipped through my hands. He has gone to set the law on me. He knows all the story of my life, and it is black enough. There is no power on earth can save me. There is no power in love to help me."

"He can be changed," she said eagerly. "He will be bought with money."

He waited a moment before he answered. "It is too late," he said, "there is nothing can stop him. He has set his heart on this thing. He cannot be changed except by death."

She merely stared at him with uncomprehending eyes. Her lips were parted dark against the pallor of the moonlit face. She had never been so strong in his desire as she was in this stricken moment.

"Perhaps there is yet time," he whispered rapidly, as if to himself more than for her ears. "I can still overtake him by a chance. And if I reach him before he gets to the town. . . ." He stopped and threw back his head. Then he stepped closer and gathered her in his arms. "I must try now," he said quickly. "I must act now. I cannot stop. Wait for me here. If I never return, you will know I have failed to find him, know that I have failed in your life. But if I return, it will be because I have made him pay the price for our happiness, and that price is the long silence."

He whirled and left her, running with the long, lunging

stride that she knew into the shades of the pine trees. She was alone.

A passing wind stirred a nearby tree till a song sparrow woke. His musical complaint troubled the night for a moment, but a little later there was nothing again in the valley save the silence and the moon.

Chapter Twenty-Seven

BENEDICT PAYS A DEBT

The moon stood high above the peaks now, and had grown small and colorless and so bright that her tracings could hardly be marked. Munroe was glad of the clear light, for the path he had to follow on his long walk to Crackens was difficult with rocks.

It was a sort of a bridle path up the valley, and traveled with slight variations the track laid down for the little railroad. But it had never received any grading, and it dipped time and again into little pools of water where Munroe more than once got wet above his shoe tops.

Yet he was in good humor. He was quite certain that Newlands was in his power now, and the memory of the scene in the drift where Newlands had double-crossed him sweetened the anticipation of the long chase with the posse over the mountains. In the end he must give in. Perhaps it would be hunger that would overcome him, or exposure would weaken him, or the strain of long travel. But in the end Newlands would be taken, and he, Munroe, would stand in front of the shackled captive and laugh.

At the picture he stopped and chuckled softly to himself. His laughter stopped suddenly, for it seemed to him that he heard a slight grating sound behind him, like the grinding of a pebble under a foot. He whirled and glanced up and down the valley. Nothing but the trees and the sharp, jutting rocks met his search. He shrugged his shoulders and resumed his march.

He commenced to sing. At first the sudden echoes from the upslanting mountains awed him back to silence, but, after he had sung a few snatches, he regained his self-confidence and his voice went true and clear through the night. He tried over bits of music-hall ballads, popular waltz songs, even chanted a few phrases of old English folk songs, for he was very happy. It would be a good game. It would be a great game, the finest sport of a lifetime.

As he passed a little winding of the path, the gurgle of moving water reminded him that he was thirsty. He found a little runlet with a short cascade that had worn away the rock below the hollow—an ideal drinking fountain. He leaned over the pool and drank deeply. He was about to rise when he heard a sound as of a step on the pebbles. He sprang sideways to his feet, and, as he leaped, he drew the hunting knife from his pocket and flung away the leather sheath that came away with it.

The act took only a breathing space, and then he stood crouched on guard in the shallow of the rock behind him. Benedict stood before him, with the moonlight plain upon his face.

"You!" breathed Munroe, and then he straightened and laughed. He was angered at its sound, it was so shaken.

Benedict drew back a pace and, as he moved, drew a knife.

Munroe could see the fingers shifting to obtain a stronger hold on the handle of the long, slim-shafted blade. He held it like a sword between his fingers, and beyond a doubt he knew how to use it. He made no answer, but ran his eyes slowly over every inch of the ground on which they stood. Yet he showed no excitement. It was a strange scene, these two prepared for battle to death in the long valley, white and peaceful with the moon and the high peaks on either side looking down upon them.

Munroe had not yet recovered his poise, but Benedict was calm and removed as if he were one looking upon a scene rather than an actor in it. He had taken on a peculiar dignity in the moment. Although he had ever been perfect in dignity, it had never seemed so entirely in place as it was now in the midst of the upleaping rocks and the silences of the mountains.

It was fitting to both Munroe and Benedict that they spoke as if they had been in a drawing room.

"Newlands has sent you to do this," Munroe announced coolly enough.

Benedict looked on him with unutterable scorn. "If Mister Newlands wished your death," he said, "he would have killed you himself . . . as a man steps on a snake. He would not dirty his hands with such dealings."

"And you have been up here waiting for days for me," went on Munroe, for he noted that Benedict was thinner and paler than usual. "It was your face that came at the window of Beatrice's cabin, eh?"

Benedict shrugged his shoulders and drew a little closer. Munroe gripped his hands to nerve himself. The thing was becoming uncanny.

"One moment, my boy," he said. "If I am to kill you here in this perfectly good moonlight, there is no reason why I should not know the causes that make the affair necessary. You lack a sense of humor, Benedict. Be a good fellow and tell me why you're so damned attentive to me now."

"Pah!" Benedict spit softly. "It soils the mouth of a Spanish gentleman to speak to such canaille."

"Tut, tut!" Munroe said, waving his left hand. "You have

always kept a black eye on me, Benedict. You don't hate me entirely at Newlands's request, eh?"

Benedict drew back again. "There is an old house on a road northward from Cordova," he said, "with white walls and green climbing vines against the walls, and very cool and pleasant in the summer. You do not remember?"

Munroe stared at him without a word.

"And in the open door of the evening a girl would sit and sometimes sing. Her voice was very light and sweet through the evening."

"By God!" cried Munroe.

"I was sure you would remember," Benedict said still very softly.

"But you . . . you?" Munroe puzzled. "What the devil had it to do with you, Benedict?"

"The girl," went on Benedict in the same voice, "was betrothed then to a young man of good family . . . Don José Alvarado. Once you bowed to him."

"A fellow with slim, upslanting mustache," Munroe agreed, and then started as he looked more closely at Benedict. "I could almost swear . . . ," he began, but stopped and shook his head.

"Yes," said Benedict. "I am José Alvarado."

"But he was rich."

"I have spent much money."

"He was noble."

"It is not hard to forget one's birth."

"He could not have left Spain."

"Only to find you, *señor*," Benedict assured, and he bowed with some dignity, but was instantly back on his guard. "For no other reason. I have forgotten to laugh all my life. I shall remember while I watch you die."

"Bah, you night-prowling cur," Munroe hissed. "Here's

for you!" He sprang with such suddenness that even agile Benedict was taken by surprise. With his left hand Munroe struck up the knife in Benedict's hand, and took a slight cut in so doing. Then as he rushed on, his chest struck Benedict's, and his right arm was free. He struck twice into Benedict's back. The first blow slipped and went awry, but he felt the second drive home solidly. He thrust Benedict away, and himself sprang back.

"You have it!" he cried. "You have it, Benedict! The wolves will come down the hills to sniff at you, my boy, before morning."

He became aware that Benedict was laughing, a little chuckle that was barely audible and that made Munroe's blood turn cold.

"I cannot die," Benedict declared, "before you. It would be impossible, *señor*. I have lived too long for this moment to fail now."

"Then take it!" Munroe yelled, and sprang again.

But this time Benedict swerved lightly before the attack. The knife-hand flashed out, and the blade struck high on Munroe's breast.

He wrenched himself away and set his teeth to keep back the cry of pain. He was badly hurt. How badly he could not tell—and it was far, far to Crackens and help.

"Damn you," Munroe groaned, "you are dying on your feet! Am I to die at the hands of a man already done for?" He attacked again madly.

They circled rapidly about the little hollow. He saw that Benedict was wavering where he stood with his feet always braced wide. But no matter how hard he strove to close with him, he met nothing save the knife. In his desperation he lost his balance twice and was badly hurt each time before he could get back on guard. Then came a slight darkening of his eyes. He thought at first that a cloud had passed over the face of the moon, but, when he looked up, he saw that it was still shining unmarred by any shadow. Then Munroe knew.

"Benedict, you dog," he muttered, "I'm badly hurt. Listen, man. There is no reason why we should fight this thing out. You are hurt as badly as I. Shall two strong men die for the sake of one small girl who ceased to live so many years ago? Bah! It is nonsense. We can bandage our wounds. We can still make it to Crackens for help."

He became aware again of the faint chuckle.

"Her memory has not died," said Benedict. "It shall not die until my death. That is coming in this hour. But you shall go before me down to hell. It is a long way, *señor,* and yet in what a little minute a strong man may travel there!"

"By God," Munroe growled, maddened at the insane coolness of his enemy and somewhat stricken with awe of him at the same moment, "it is you who shall show the way!"

He closed again, thrusting and cutting. More than once he found a mark for his blows. More than once a burning pang told him that he was paid in full for the damage he had done.

Then the dimness that had been threatening his eyes grew suddenly black. He went reeling back awkwardly like a man who rises from a position which he has held for a long time. He dropped very close to the runlet. Benedict made toward him with fumbling steps, then his legs gave way beneath him, and he fell upon his face.

He lay senseless only for a short moment. It was as if the purpose in his heart was for the moment as strong as the force of death. A quiver passed through his body; the head raised slightly; then he drew himself painfully upon his hands and knees and crawled toward Munroe.

Munroe lay fallen upon his back with his face turned into

235

the moonlight, and he was quite insensible. For a time Benedict watched his face. Then he reached into the runlet and from the palm of his hand dashed a shower of cold water upon Munroe. The hands of the latter clenched, and then his eyes opened.

"What is it?" he muttered, and then groaned as the pain of his wounds brought him back to full consciousness.

Benedict drew himself a little higher and managed to seat himself with his back against the rock and his arms braced on each side to support himself erect as he sat, peering into Munroe's face.

"Benedict," Munroe whispered, "there is yet time. I am bleeding to death, but there is yet time. Tear my shirt into strips and . . . I tell you, you fool, that I cannot die. There is too much left for me to do."

"Yes," Benedict said, and the chuckle ran like a little accompaniment between his words. "You have still to die and go to hell with me. I shall go at your heels to see that you do not cheat the devil."

"You are mad," groaned Munroe, "and you'll pay the price."

"No," Benedict stated quietly. "I am paid in full now for many years of hell. It is very pleasant to sit here and watch your face, *señor.*

Munroe closed his eyes as the faintness came over him again. With a great effort Benedict leaned again into the runlet and scooped up water, which he threw in the dying man's face.

"Above all," he went on, "it is pleasant to think how this sight will amuse Mister Newlands, for he knows that dead men never talk, *señor.*"

He saw a spasm of fury contort Munroe's face.

"Damn you," whispered Munroe, "you are a fiend, not a

man." He made an effort to rise, but he could barely lift his head.

"So," murmured Benedict. "So. Rest easy, *señor*. You shall never stand up again. But it is very pleasant to die here in the full moon. It is very pleasant. Yes, I am moved to laughter. I have the right to laugh, eh, *señor?* Have you not failed in all the ways of your life? And have I not been the cause?"

Again the ghostly chuckle sounded silver through the moonlight, and passed away into the murmur of the dripping water.

Munroe moved his lips to answer, but no words came, and only fear stood in his eyes as he watched the Spaniard.

"Yes," went on Benedict, "it is very pleasant here. It reminds me deeply of those other evenings in Cordova. Ah, it is a lovely city. I have seen its towers like a vision against the red west. And I have seen a girl sitting in the door of her father's house on such a night. Her face was lovely then, was it not, *señor?*"

But when he looked for an answer, he saw that Munroe's eyes were turned vacantly up to the moon. Benedict's head fell slowly back upon his shoulders and rested against the rock. His whole body slumped a little forward, and his eyes also went up to the sky.

"It is not hard," Benedict whispered. "It is not hard to die when one can laugh. It is a gentle thing."

And when death came there was a smile of content upon his lips.

So it was that Newlands came upon them. He had run hard from the moment he left Beatrice, and, as he swerved heavily around the sharp bend, his eye caught the two shadows in the moonlight. And then he saw the dull eyes of

Benedict fixed upon him, forever without recognition.

He stood dazed for a little moment, and the splash and whisper of the runlet dropped slowly through his thoughts. To Munroe's body he gave only a glance.

He knew that Munroe had, indeed, paid the price of his happiness in full. But suddenly that happiness drew far away and seemed to matter nothing before this other and larger thing.

So Newlands knelt in front of Benedict for a long time and watched his face, how it was touched by the quiet smile and how it was shadowed by the moon.

He took the body at last and laid it carefully at full length with the arms at the sides. Then he closed the eyes. He would have covered his face, but it seemed to him a moment later that it would be better to leave the dignity of his face naked to the sky.

When he took the road back toward the Victory Mine, he did not hurry, and his head was bowed toward the ground. Yet he was not possessed of sadness, only of an exceedingly great wonder.

RONICKY DOONE

First Time In Paperback!

"Brand is a topnotcher!"
—New York Times

Doone's name is famous throughout the Old West. From Tombstone to Sonora he's won the respect of every law-abiding citizen—and the hatred of every bushwhacking bandit. But Bill Gregg isn't one to let a living legend get in his way, and he'll shoot Doone dead as soon as look at him. What nobody tells Gregg is that Doone doesn't enjoy living his hard-riding, rip-roaring life unless he takes a chance on losing it once in a while.

_3738-6 $3.99 US/$4.99 CAN

Dorchester Publishing Co., Inc.
P.O. Box 6640
Wayne, PA 19087-8640

Please add $1.75 for shipping and handling for the first book and $.50 for each book thereafter. NY, NYC, and PA residents, please add appropriate sales tax. No cash, stamps, or C.O.D.s. All orders shipped within 6 weeks via postal service book rate. Canadian orders require $2.00 extra postage and must be paid in U.S. dollars through a U.S. banking facility.

Name_____

Address_____

City_____ State_____ Zip_____

I have enclosed $_____ in payment for the checked book(s).

Payment <u>must</u> accompany all orders. ☐ Please send a free catalog.